A MAIDEN IN DISTRESS

"Hand over the lass, and we'll leave ye to your affairs."

Lachlan wondered what on earth a wee lass could have done to incur the wrath of this mob. Two of the villagers had their daggers drawn, four more wielded spades, and all of them had feverish fire in their eyes. He didn't care if the woman had butchered their livestock and set their fields on fire. 'Twas an unfair fight, and he didn't like unfair fights.

"Lass?" he dared them. "What lass?"

THE OUTCAST

The Prequel Novella to The Scottish Lasses

OTHER BOOKS BY GLYNNIS CAMPBELL

THE WARRIOR MAIDS OF RIVENLOCH
The Shipwreck (novella)
Lady Danger
Captive Heart
Knight's Prize

THE KNIGHTS OF DE WARE
The Handfasting (novella)
My Champion
My Warrior
My Hero

MEDIEVAL OUTLAWS
Danger's Kiss
Passion's Exile

THE SCOTTISH LASSES
The Outcast (novella)
MacFarland's Lass
MacAdam's Lass

THE CALIFORNIA LEGENDS
Native Gold
Native Wolf

ACKNOWLEDGMENTS

Special thanks to:

Tanya and Laurin for taking a wary Hobbit
on a special journey,

Lauren Royal for being a genius and a cheerleader,

my sister Jewels of Historical Romance
for their loving support,

The Crown Jewels—best street team on the planet,

Charlie Hunnam and Amy Acker for inspiration,

and my husband Rich
for fun-filled geeky discussions

For wounded warriors and incurable nerds

everywhere...

I love you just the way you are.

CHAPTER 1

Keirfield, Scotland
Late November, 1542

Biera blew out a frosty breath and narrowed her one good eye at the cottage door.

Never had she felt so full of doubt. For hundreds of years the wise old crone had served as the Guardian of the Winter Stone. She'd borne the honorable burden of passing the treasure from Keeper to Keeper all through the ages. And she'd never failed to find the right Keeper for the precious relic.

But this time, something felt wrong.

Still, the rare round crystal in the wooden claw of her staff glowed with soft assurance, illuminating the snowflakes falling gently in the dark around her. She lifted the staff for a third time to rap on the door.

Finally she heard a shuffling scrape from within the

cottage. After a long moment, the door creaked open a few inches.

Through the crack, a scruffy blond-headed giant frowned down at her with groggy, bloodshot eyes of gray. She could smell the whisky on him.

She frowned back. His hair was the wrong color. His eyes were the wrong shade.

Also wrong were the features of the second head that suddenly jutted out just below his—grizzled gray hair with brown eyes. Worse, they belonged to a gigantic slobbering deerhound.

She grimaced.

There wasn't much time. The new queen was about to be born—the old king about to die. The Scottish army had just suffered a harrowing defeat at the Battle of Solway Moss. The fate of all Scotland resided in the Winter Stone. Putting it into the right hands was crucial.

Biera tightened her grip on the staff and lifted a hopeful brow. "Anyone else livin' here?"

Lachlan squeezed his eyes shut. A moment ago, he'd been asleep and dreaming. Before that, he'd been drunk. 'Twas hard to tell anymore what was real and what wasn't. But when he opened his eyes again, the old crone was still there.

"God's bones, woman," he growled. "What are ye doin' out on a night like this? Ye'll catch your death o'—"

"Time's a-wastin'," she interjected, dismissing him

with an irritated wave of her hand. "Aye or nae? Is there another livin' here?"

Lachlan Mar wasn't in the habit of receiving visitors ever, let alone at this ungodly hour. Hell, he wasn't even dressed. He'd managed to slip a linen shirt over his head, and he'd pulled on his trews, but he hadn't bothered lacing them, and he didn't know where his doublet had gone.

He sighed. He knew he shouldn't have answered the door. Anyone who'd wander the woods alone on a snowy winter's eve had to be daft.

What had she asked him—whether anyone else lived here?

Someone else *had* lived here, but no more. Margaret had fled less than a fortnight after Lachlan came home from the war.

"A couple o' mice maybe," he grunted, half hoping to scare the woman off.

'Twas against his nature to let people into his cottage. 'Twas his refuge, his escape, a place he could drink away his troubles and hide from his past.

But the old woman didn't look like she was leaving any time soon.

And as indifferent as he wanted to be, 'twas also against his nature to let people freeze to death on his threshold.

He rested his forehead against the edge of the door. 'Twould only be till morn, he supposed. He'd let her warm her bones by the fire and then send her on her way at daylight. And that would be that.

Besides, 'twasn't as if she'd mock his...deformity. A one-eyed woman could hardly make a fuss over a one-legged man.

He took hold of Campbell's collar to keep the hound from charging and opened the door wider.

Her gaze immediately flew to his crutch and his abbreviated leg, and she gasped.

"Ye're crippled?" she bluntly exclaimed, then continued in a mutter, "Nae, that canna be right. Ye dinna have the right features. And ye're sotted to boot. Somethin's gone awry."

He clenched his jaw, tamping down the urge to tell her those were rather bold words coming from a withered, one-eyed old crone. At least she wasn't throwing rocks at him like the village lads used to...before he'd acquired his fearsome deerhound.

Finally sighing in surrender, he tried to coax her forward with a nod of his head. "Come in out o' the cold, grandmother, ere the frost cracks your frail bones."

A keen twinkle appeared in her eye then, and she let out a soft cackle. "These frail bones have withstood a thousand fierce winters. 'Twould take more than a wee bit o' snow to pierce my hide."

She was definitely daft, he decided. She looked ancient, aye, but a thousand winters? She couldn't be more than seventy years old. And no one could long endure the cold of a Scottish winter without the benefit of shelter. He was shivering just from the flurry of snowflakes that had swept in through the door. Even his hound had known enough to come in for the night.

Lachlan perused the crone slowly from the top of her woolen hood to the tips of her snow-covered boots as she studied him in return. Then he noticed the wooden staff she was holding. The claw at the top of it held a frosty white crystal in the shape of a perfect sphere. 'Twas glowing with a strange light.

At first he thought it must be his imagination. Sometimes when he'd been drinking, he saw things that weren't real. Maybe the old woman wasn't real either.

Then she made a grab for his arm, nearly knocking the crutch out from under him, dispelling that notion.

"Give me your hand," she commanded.

Stunned by her suddenly forceful manner, he froze.

"Your hand!" she insisted.

He unfurled his fist, and she tipped the staff toward him. The claw released, dropping the heavy, round crystal into his palm. It was cold and polished smooth, a milky white stone almost as large as a hen's egg.

Her eye snapped as she asked him, "Will ye be the one to take the Winter Stone to its rightful Keeper?"

He scowled. What was the woman blathering about? Winter Stone? Rightful Keeper? That sounded suspiciously like it might involve a journey. Was she jesting? On one leg, Lachlan could scarcely walk to the spring and back, let alone embark on a journey to deliver some trinket for her.

"Will ye?" she demanded, shaking his arm roughly. For a wee woman, she was certainly strong. Perhaps madness did that to a person. "Answer me!" she spat, her gaze ferocious.

The corners of his mouth turned down. He supposed he wouldn't be able to pry his arm from her grip until he gave her an answer. He grumbled, "Aye. Why not? I'll take it."

"To its rightful heir? The one with dark hair and bright green eyes?"

"Aye. Fine." That should assuage the mad crone.

The old woman seized his hand then and peered closely at the stone. It seemed to throw off a curious rosy shimmer as she did so. Apparently satisfied by what she'd glimpsed, she nodded and grunted and closed his fingers around the stone.

"Then I'll be off," she stated. "'Tis in your hands now. Keep it safe. 'Tisn't a thing to take lightly. The Winter Stone has the power to change your fate."

"My fate, ach, o' course, I see," he said to placate her. Then he turned aside for a moment to pull Campbell out of the way. "Now that that's settled, be a good lass. Come in and warm yourself by the—"

When he turned back, she was gone, vanished like mist in the snowy night. If not for the milky round stone in his palm, he might have believed he'd imagined the whole encounter.

He called out loudly. He even sent Campbell to search for her, not relishing the idea of finding a dead woman in front of his cottage on the morrow. But the deerhound came ambling back with his head lowered in guilt, unable to find her.

"That's all right, lad." Lachlan scratched the hound behind his ears. "Ye did your best." He squinted into the

dark night, but 'twas impossible to see more than a few yards. "God willin', she'll find her way to shelter." Under his breath, he added, "Or we'll be thawin' her carcass out come morn." With that unsavory thought, he tossed the round stone out the door and into the snow.

Campbell immediately raced outside after it.

"Nae, lad!"

His command had no effect. The hound spent several moments nosing around in the snow until he found the bauble, picked it up, and came trotting back to the cottage, depositing it on the flagstone floor before Lachlan.

Lachlan gave him a rueful smile. He supposed the poor pup was starved for play. A man with a missing leg was not the ideal companion for a hound accustomed to running down deer.

Maybe he should be kind to the faithful beast and hand him over to someone who could exercise him properly...someone who was still useful...someone with two legs.

A familiar sharp twinge seized his heart, taking him by surprise. After three months, he thought he'd be used to his infirmity, used to the frustration and hopelessness. But his wounds still ached. The real pain of his useless existence gnawed at him daily, just like the false pain of his missing limb.

He sniffed sharply, then picked up the stone and tossed it once in his palm. It looked changed somehow, its rosy glow darkened to a muddy shade. But change his fate? Nothing could do that. With a bitter oath, he cast the thing away, back into the frozen night.

Before he could stop the hound, Campbell bounded out the door and after it again.

Lachlan shook his head at the fool dog. Maybe the thick-furred hound could stand the cold, but *he* was beginning to shiver, standing in the open doorway in nothing but his trews and his linen shirt. And Campbell would doubtless bring half the snowdrifts back into the cottage with him when he returned.

The hound again brought the stone between his teeth, his panting making fog in the chill air. He lowered his head and set his treasure gently on the floor once more.

"'Tisn't a game, lad," Lachlan explained, retrieving the stone. "Sit." The hound obeyed. "Stay." He gave the hound a stern look, and then heaved the stone as far as he could one last time.

To his astonishment, the normally obedient deerhound leaped up and out the doorway, pushing aside the door when Lachlan tried to close it, almost upending his master in the process.

"Campbell!" Lachlan shouted. "What the devil?"

He didn't know what had gotten into the dog. Campbell always followed his master's commands. He was a faithful beast and served Lachlan well, hunting down game to keep them both fed.

But it seemed as if a strange wind had blown in with the snowstorm, disturbing the natural order of things. What else could explain a midnight visit from a one-eyed crone, her curious glowing crystal, the woman's sudden disappearance, and now his disobedient dog? Something unusual was definitely in the air.

"Campbell!" he called again. He'd thrown the stone a good distance, and he feared his persistent hound might freeze himself looking for it.

But just about the time he'd decided he was going to have to grab his cloak and limp after the dog, Campbell trotted up proudly with his prize, thoughtfully shaking the snow off of his fur before he entered the cottage.

Lachlan smirked. "Fine." He bent to pick up the stone. He would have sworn it glinted blue for an instant before he closed his hand around it and shut the door against the swirling snowflakes. "We'll leave it here then." He hobbled over to the hearth and set the piece on the stone mantel, where it seemed to wink at him. He frowned. "Just don't expect it to change your fate, lad," he said, giving the hound a scratch on his damp head. "I'm afraid ye're stuck with me."

Campbell looked satisfied with that. He circled three times and settled down before the dwindling fire.

Lachlan couldn't settle down so easily. He poked at the coals, adding another log and stirring the fire back to life, igniting his own whirling thoughts as well.

As mad as the crone had seemed, he was haunted by her promise. He wished he *could* change his fate. Indeed, he wished he'd died along with his brothers three months ago at Haddon Rig.

That wish brought back painful memories, memories he'd fought hard to suppress. But tonight, with the world a bleak, frozen, isolated place, they hit him full-force. His throat ached with grief as angry tears welled in his eyes.

The words came to him as they always did.

He should be dead.

His brothers were dead—all four of them. They'd been killed on that bloody battlefield, slain by English blades, their bodies trampled beneath English horses. Lachlan had promised his father he'd look out for them, and he'd failed.

Why had he been spared? Why hadn't he died in glorious battle with them instead of suffering a grievous wound and living in lonely exile as half a man?

Children feared him. Men pitied him. And women? They recoiled from him, as his dear Margaret had, sickened by his hideous disfigurement.

This wasn't surviving. 'Twas punishment.

He *should* be dead.

He lowered himself onto his bed and stared into the harsh flames. There was only one way to cope with these fits of melancholy that turned him from the brave soldier he'd once been into the weepy, self-pitying wretch he was now.

He eyed the jack of whisky he'd left on the table. There was enough left to bring him drunken oblivion, maybe enough to make him forget for one night the horrific Battle of Haddon Rig.

CHAPTER 2

Alisoune Hay's heart pounded painfully. They were coming after her. She wheezed through her burning lungs, cursing her tight stomacher, and squinted in the bright morning sunlight as she floundered through the thick fallen snow. Her satchel flopped against her thigh as she hoisted her sodden skirts up with one hand and held her spectacles onto her nose with the other.

She could hear the irate shouts of the townsfolk as they pursued her. Some of them were calling her witch. Some were calling her blasphemer. And some of them were calling her things she pretended not to hear.

'Twasn't the first time she'd earned the disapproval of an entire town. As her parents had oft remarked, Alisoune's mouth was even bigger than her brain. And that was saying something.

Usually the people in the towns she passed through dismissed her opinions as the brash ravings of an

impertinent young lass. But this time they'd taken her more seriously. This time, according to the awful red-haired priest who'd instigated the hasty proceedings against her, she'd spoken against common wisdom, God's will, and the very nature of the known world.

But that had been precisely her point. The world was *not* known. In fact, science had barely scratched the surface of the vast realm of knowledge. How could man possibly pretend to know everything about the universe?

She suddenly stumbled over her dark green skirts and fell face-down in the snow. She heard a shout behind her and felt an instant of panic as the ground blurred in her vision. Patting feverishly about with her hand, she finally located her fallen spectacles and perched them again on her nose. They were wet and covered with snowflakes, but at least she could see.

Scrambling to her feet, she surged forward. She hadn't expected the crowd to follow her so far. And by their growing rage, it seemed they intended to do something more dire than merely run her out of town.

Now that her parents had gone to France and left the business to Alisoune, she had no one to placate the townsfolk and assuage their anger. She'd already tried to explain herself in a reasonable fashion and even resorted to offering the priest money to withdraw his claim. But that had only gotten her into more trouble.

"Burn the witch!" she heard in the distance.

Her breath caught, and she tried to slog faster through the snow, despite the cold, throbbing ache in her chest. They couldn't be serious. Burn her?

What could she do? Where could she go? She quickly cataloged her options.

She had no horse, no cart. There was no church nearby for sanctuary. There wasn't even a troupe of players or a group of pilgrims to vanish into, which was her usual mode of safe transportation from town to town.

If only she owned a pair of those wooden planks the Danish soldiers attached to their feet, she thought, she might be able to glide across the snow and lose her pursuers.

Or even better...one of those man-carrying kites invented by the ancient Chinese that could allow a person to fly over the treetops.

But she had neither. And no matter how diligently she tried to employ that big brain of hers, she could think of no plausible escape.

She certainly didn't want to be burned at the stake as a witch. 'Twas an unpleasant way to die, especially if the wood didn't create enough smoke to asphyxiate her first and she was forced to endure the flesh-scorching heat of the flames.

She let out an involuntary squeak of remorse. Why did she always have to think in such exquisite detail? Sometimes she wished her brain wasn't quite so big and that she could wool-gather her way through life like more simpleminded lasses, without a care.

The shouting grew louder, and she increased her pace, wincing at the stitch in her side. But she'd already done the calculations. Despite her long legs, the weight of her

skirts gave the men following her at least a fifty percent advantage when it came to speed. They'd catch up to her in a matter of moments.

Then she saw something she hadn't figured into the equation—a seemingly abandoned cottage nestled at the edge of the forest.

Maybe she could hide there.

Her instincts for survival renewed, she bolted toward the place.

Before she'd gone two yards, the door of the cottage opened wide, and out charged a great gray beast. As if propelled by rockets, it began running straight toward her.

She gasped. When it leaped at her, all she saw was a scruffy face full of gray fur and a huge gaping maw full of sharp teeth. The animal knocked her down with its paws. Once she'd fallen softly onto the snow, it began to mercilessly lick her face.

It never hurt her. In fact, when the hound—which was the biggest dog she'd ever seen—heard the men yelling in the distance, it growled deep in its throat and nudged her as if telling her to get up and move before they arrived.

She grabbed her spectacles and satchel and staggered forward. The hound enthusiastically bounded around her, guiding her toward the cottage.

At the threshold, she glanced back once to see that the mob of a dozen or so men had spotted her. They bolted forward, their snapping cloaks and foul mood a dark contrast to the bright snow.

Then she swept into the cottage with the dog, slamming the door behind her.

Lachlan, still half-asleep, winced and groaned as the cottage shook from the impact of the door slamming. He opened one eye. The other felt like it was sealed shut. His mouth was as dry as plaster. And his head throbbed from the aftereffects of too much whisky.

"Campbell," he moaned. Over the past few weeks, the hound had somehow learned how to open the latch on the cottage door and tended to come and go as he pleased.

But the scuffling didn't quite sound like his hound. And when Lachlan managed to pry open his other eye, both eyes went suddenly wide at the sight before him.

Instinctively, he rose up on his elbows. "Who are *ye?*"

The tall young woman in the green gown blinked in surprise, as if she didn't expect to see anyone actually inhabiting the cottage. At least he *thought* she blinked. 'Twas hard to tell, because her eyes were shielded by two round pieces of glass perched atop her nose.

Before she could answer him, there was a loud pounding at the door. She dove for the bed, sailing over him to wriggle beneath the bed linens and pull the sheepskin coverlet over her head.

He was still reeling in shock at her boldness when the pounding came again, accompanied by irate shouts.

She started at the sound, and he felt her cold, naked leg brush against his as her small icy fist burrowed beneath his hip.

He glanced down at the shivering mound of sheepskin beside him. The woman was clearly hiding from whoever was outside. And whoever was outside clearly knew she was here. The last thing Lachlan needed was to get caught in the crossfire.

The pounding resumed, louder this time, and the woman peeked out long enough to plead with him in an urgent whisper. "I beg ye, sir, hide me. I fear they mean to burn me at the stake." She was pale from the cold, but her cheeks were rosy from exertion, and she was quivering like a cornered mouse. Indeed, with her longish nose and those big spectacles, she looked a bit like a mouse. "Please, sir, please. Keep me safe."

Then he frowned. *Keep her safe.* He was the last person to be trusted to keep someone safe. His brothers had depended on him to keep them safe. Four gravestones were proof of how that had ended.

But Campbell was staring expectantly at the door. And Lachlan knew he had to answer it. If whoever was outside intended to burn the woman at the stake, they might be carrying torches even now. And they might decide to make quick work of it by setting his whole cottage on fire.

With as little fuss as possible, Lachlan eased his right leg over the edge of the bed, tucked his crutch under his left arm, and pushed up. As usual, he staggered, and his head started throbbing, but he managed to regain his balance and limp over to the doorway.

He snatched open the door. "What do ye want?" he demanded harshly.

At least a dozen townsmen crowded together, trying to peer past him into the one-room cottage. He knew the men, though in the last three months since he'd moved back to Keirfield, he'd kept mostly to himself. Now—whether 'twas due to his rough and ragged appearance, his stern scowl, or his growling hound—nobody answered his question.

"Ye hauled me out o' bed with your infernal racket," he bit out. "So what do ye want?"

Finally, Father Ninian, the red-haired parish priest, gathered up enough courage to raise his quivering double-chin, demanding, "Hand over the lass, and we'll leave ye to your affairs."

Lachlan wondered what on earth a wee lass could have done to incur the wrath of this mob. Two of the villagers had their daggers drawn, four more wielded spades, and all of them had feverish fire in their eyes. He didn't care if the woman had butchered their livestock and set their fields on fire. 'Twas an unfair fight, and he didn't like unfair fights.

"Lass?" he dared them. "What lass?"

The father narrowed his pale blue eyes and began shuddering with rage. "Ye know very well," he growled. "We saw her run in here."

Lachlan looked down from a considerable height on all of the men. "Did ye?"

The townsfolk muttered in agreement.

He cast a quick backward glance at his bed to assure the lass was well-hidden. Then he opened the door far enough for them to see the interior of his cottage. "Well, I don't see her now. Do ye?"

Father Ninian charged forward, elbowing aside his fellows. "Out o' my way. I'll find that Satan's spawn."

The deerhound growled.

"I wouldn't do that if I were ye," Lachlan warned. "I've seen Campbell here tear a man limb from limb."

'Twasn't at all true. Campbell was keen for rabbit and could take down a small deer. But he mostly just growled at strangers.

Still, Father Ninian didn't know that. So for the sake of caution, the priest backed away. Then he stabbed a threatening finger at Lachlan and snarled, "Ye mark my words, Mar, 'tisn't the end of it. Ye're harborin' a daughter o' the devil, and I mean to see her punished for her blasphemy."

With that, the father spun on his heel, and the mob marched off with him, grumbling empty threats to the air as they made their way across the rutted snow.

Lachlan closed the door and turned back to the bed. Blasphemy? Daughter of the devil? God's eyes, what had the woman done? Maybe he'd made a mistake, not turning her over to them.

"They're gone," he said cautiously. "Ye're safe."

Tentative fingers crept out from under the sheepskin. Almost without knowing he did so, Lachlan braced himself for her gasp. Women always gasped when they first saw him, even those who tried to be polite.

When she threw back the sheepskin all at once, her spectacles went flying. But her face beamed as she sat up with a broad, grateful grin.

Lachlan arched a brow in surprise. Now that he could

see all of her clearly, he decided that while she might be a trifle mouse-like, she wasn't an unattractive lass. Her hair was the color of dark, wet wood. Her smile was soft and sweet. And her eyes reminded him of the first tender grass of spring.

Indeed, he thought with mild irritation, she glowed like a beam of sunshine—a ray of blinding white light to awaken him from his comfortable, numb slumber.

He exhaled. She seemed like she might be the cheery sort who'd try to drag him, kicking and screaming, into her bright world, a world in which he no longer belonged.

"Oh, sir, ye were magnificent!" she crowed, patting the feather-filled mattress for her lost spectacles. "Threatenin' them with your hound. But that big, droolin' beast wouldn't harm a flea, would he?"

"Campbell? Nae," he grunted, eyeing her spectacles on the floor.

"I can't thank ye enough, kind sir." She hadn't gasped yet, but maybe without her spectacles she was blind. "I owe ye my life."

He stiffened, reminded of the dead men who'd trusted him with their lives.

She continued to rummage through the blankets for her spectacles. Lachlan was in no great hurry to return them to her. "If it hadn't been for your lovely hound and your quick—"

He snorted.

"What?" she asked.

"Lovely?"

"He *is* lovely," she said with a coy smile. "And so are ye...for keepin' me safe."

There 'twas again, that phrase—*keeping her safe.* Those were the same words the old crone had used for the strange crystal. *Keep it safe.* He glanced over at the mantel. The stone was still there, safe for the moment.

As for the lass, she hadn't gasped yet. In fact, she'd just called him lovely. Now he *knew* she was blind.

He couldn't continue to let her search in vain. Besides, though he'd held off the angry mob for the moment, he didn't want to harbor a fugitive, no matter how bonnie she was. 'Twas probably best she get her gasping over with and go on her way.

Leaning on his crutch, he bent down to retrieve her spectacles and put them into her hands, and then hobbled toward the hearth.

"Oh, thank ye," she said, fumbling them back onto her nose. "Honestly, ye'd think I'd told the priest that the world was flat or some such..."

By her hesitation, he knew she'd spotted his deformity. But she didn't gasp. Instead, to his amazement, she cooed in wonder.

"Ahh, ye've got a missin' limb!" She scrambled to perch on the edge of the bed and began chattering with rapt enthusiasm. "A most fascinatin' circumstance! Ye can sometimes feel it as though 'tis still there, can't ye? 'Tis called phantom pain. Benedetti believes that nerves are like the roots of a tree. Yet no one has been able to discover why, when the root is cut, the sensation o' the

limb remains long after..." She trailed off at the sight of his furrowed brow. "Oh, I'm sorry. I'm bein' impolite, aren't I?"

She *was* being terribly blunt. But for some reason it didn't trouble him. She seemed genuinely interested in his condition and, to his consternation, not at all appalled by it.

She fidgeted with the satchel that was still draped diagonally over one shoulder. "My mother always said I was cursed with too much curiosity and candor. She said I had no stopper on the keg o' my thoughts. Anyway, I didn't mean to offend ye, especially after all ye've—"

"Are ye hungry?" he asked suddenly, and then just as suddenly regretted his invitation. What the devil was he thinking? He barely had two sticks to rub together, let alone the wherewithal to entertain company. Besides, hadn't he just decided against harboring a fugitive?

A quick lick of her lips gave her away, but she said, "I don't wish to impose."

"'Tis no imposition," he lied. Even as he spoke the words, he thought he must be a fool for letting her linger. After all, no good could possibly come of it.

He limped over to the hearth and coaxed the smoldering coals to waken. Then he rummaged in his cupboard for his store of oats and raided the bowl of apples sitting on the shelf beneath it.

She patted her knees, summoning Campbell to her. Scratching the spoiled beast's shaggy head, she murmured to him. "That's a good canine. If ye vow not to

tear me limb from limb, I'll share my breakfast with ye."

The hound licked her face, knocking her spectacles askew, and she giggled.

Somewhere deep inside, Lachlan felt his frozen heart thaw a little at her laughter. 'Twas a lovely sound, one he hadn't heard in a long while. It felt like the comforting heat of a winter's bath on a frosty day...which reminded him...it had been a week or more since he'd had a bath.

He had little reason to bathe. Margaret had left him. He saw no one else. He seldom went out. Besides, on one leg, 'twas an ordeal to fetch enough water for a bath.

He probably stank. His clothes were filthy. His overlong hair hung like tangled straw. He hadn't bothered to trim his beard in weeks.

Suddenly self-conscious, he pulled together his doublet and buttoned it over his rumpled linen shirt. He tucked his unruly hair behind his ears and dipped into the bucket of water to one side of the hearth, giving his face a quick scrub and rinsing out his mouth. Then, silently cursing himself for even caring, he set to work at the wooden table, preparing the oats and peeling and cutting the apple, occasionally casting sidelong glances at the lass, who seemed to be making herself at home in his shabby hovel.

She was almost as tall as he was, a bonnie, scrawny, gangly bit of a thing with narrow shoulders and a neck no bigger than the trunk of a sapling. Much of the long, dark hair she'd pulled back into a braid had come loose, and wild tendrils curled down her cheeks and across her small bosom. Her eyes were large and of a most unusual

green that almost seemed to glow. But that might be due to the magnifying lenses of the spectacles.

What made his heart catch was her smile. 'Twas a smile of gratitude as she wordlessly thanked him for making her breakfast, a smile of acceptance as she perused his rundown cottage, a smile of pure joy as she fawned over his hound.

How anyone could think the bonnie angel before him was the daughter of the devil, Lachlan couldn't imagine. But he supposed he should investigate further.

CHAPTER 3

Alisoune had never seen a cottage, or a man, so woefully neglected. He must live on his own, she decided, for no woman she knew would let a place, or a husband, become so untidy.

Cobwebs hung from every corner. Dust covered every surface. The ash was thick in the fireplace. And there were enough crumbs on the kitchen shelves and on the flagstone floor to sustain a healthy colony of mice.

Of course, it must be challenging to keep a house clean when one was forced to move about on one leg, no matter how otherwise robust one was.

The man was definitely robust. Though his linen shirt and trews were crumpled and his doublet stained, and though he was in sorry need of a bath and a shave, he was in splendid physical condition. Few men could match Alisoune's height, but this one was over six feet tall by her estimates, broad of chest and brawny of build. No doubt he'd developed those wide, muscular

shoulders using a crutch to compensate for his missing leg.

As far as how he'd lost it... By the sword, shield, and armor tossed into one of the corners, she deduced he'd been a soldier. Wounds like that happened all the time when men insisted on battling with barbaric weapons like sharpened claymores.

But she had no scientific explanation for the way her heart was pulsing unnaturally as she watched him prepare the porridge. Something about the way his disheveled hair framed his bearded jaw...his muscled forearms hung the heavy iron pot over the fire with ease...his silver eyes narrowed at the flickering flames...made her blood feel suddenly warm and her heart beat a wee bit fast.

'Twasn't an altogether unpleasant feeling, and she was content to have it continue.

When the porridge began to simmer, he stirred the apples into the pot and asked casually, "So how did ye manage to incur the wrath o' the good people o' Keirfield?" He popped a stray bit of apple into his mouth and chewed.

She eyed him uncertainly. There had been a sardonic edge to his voice as he said "good people," but she didn't want to risk incurring his wrath as she had theirs. Sometimes the things Alisoune found interesting, others found deeply disturbing.

"'Twas naught," she said with an insincere shrug. "I was only passin' on a kernel o' knowledge...somethin' that could change the manner in which we view the entire universe. That's all."

He stopped chewing and stirring and arched dubious brows at her. "What?"

She couldn't help herself then. 'Twas such an exciting piece of news. Keeping it secret was harder than keeping a jack in its box. Her eyes lit up as she told him about Copernicus's latest theory. "'Tis quite possible—highly likely, in fact—that 'tis not the Earth which is at the center of our galaxy, but indeed the Sun, and that all the planets revolve around it."

He swallowed the bit of apple, and his expression went from dubious to amused. But 'twasn't the sort of amused scorn to which she'd grown accustomed. 'Twas more like amused fascination. "Ye think so?"

"*Copernicus* thinks so."

He resumed stirring. "Copernicus."

"Aye, the Prussian astronomer. 'Tis his heliocentric hypothesis."

He didn't even try to repeat that. "How do ye know about matters of astronomy?"

She straightened with pride and gave him a conspiratorial wink. "A woman o' my profession has access to all sorts o' men in high places."

His smile froze. His spoon suddenly slipped, and he burned his finger on the pot's rim. Then, quickly popping the injured digit into his mouth, he mumbled, "Your...profession?"

"Aye." She hefted up her satchel. "I'm a spectacle-seller."

He seemed relieved. "A spectacle-seller. Oh. Aye. O' course."

"I've sold spectacles to some o' the most esteemed academics in Scotland," she said proudly.

"Is that so?"

"Aye. Would ye like to see them?"

He gave her a puzzled frown. "The academics?"

"Nay," she chided with a giggle. "My spectacles."

A soft shimmer came into his gray eyes, like a candle appearing in the fog, as she saw he was only jesting with her.

Nobody ever jested with her. People usually thought she wasn't quite right in the head. The fact that he was treating her like an ordinary person suffused her with a sweet warmth.

Lachlan knew he shouldn't encourage the lass. 'Twas pointless. Besides, he needed to send her away before...before he started getting second thoughts about sending her away.

Still, when she looked at him with that damned sunny gleam in her eyes, how could he resist? He left the wooden spoon in the pot, wedged the crutch under his arm, and hobbled toward the bed.

She popped up, pulled a small box out of her satchel, and opened it. A neat row of spectacles were nestled inside, between strips of cloth which he presumed protected the glass from scratches.

"The lenses come in various strengths, dependin' on the need," she explained. "Most buy cheap leather frames, which can be replaced when they wear thin. But for the

more affluent patron, they're made o' metal or ox bone or, like this pair…" She carefully lifted out a special pair of spectacles and handed them to him. "Polished horn."

Lachlan pretended to admire the spectacles. But in truth, he found the lass showing them to him to be far more intriguing. As he handed them back to her, he tried again to see through the spectacles she was wearing. Her eyes had looked grass green before. But now they seemed to twinkle like emeralds.

She looked up to catch him staring. "Ah, ye've noticed my own spectacles," she guessed incorrectly. "And ye probably want to know why the spectacle-seller wears simple leather frames." She slipped him a confiding grin. "I'll tell ye a wee secret. In fact, the true value is in the lenses. 'Tis no easy task…"

She halted, probably because he was indeed staring at her, unable to tear his gaze away from her smiling face. How long had it been since a woman had looked at him without cringing in horror?

"No easy task," she repeated, "findin' the perfect magnification." Her eyelids dipped, and she gulped, speaking more slowly. "And once ye do…"

She was staring back at him now. Her eyes looked like deep verdant pools. "'Tis best to hold onto them," she said, her voice growing softer, "and…and…'

He swallowed hard. 'Twas so rare—a moment like this when he didn't feel like the village monster, when he felt like a man, whole and hale—that he didn't want it to end. He was afraid to move, afraid to speak, afraid to look away. He scarcely breathed the word. "And?"

"And replace the frames when they're..." she trailed off, lowering the spectacles in her hand.

He didn't think. He didn't plan. He simply reached up and gently removed the spectacles from her nose and looked deep into her eyes. Apple green. Fern green. The green of new leaves in May and soft moss in clear pools.

His gaze lowered then to her rosy lips. How long had it been since he'd had that sweet taste, since he'd felt the soft caress of a woman? It seemed an eternity since he'd shared a kiss...and he doubted he'd ever have another chance.

But his heart squeezed in pain even as he dared to hope. No matter how great his hunger, this lass wasn't his to have. He didn't deserve such sweetness anyway. And 'twas not his way to force himself upon a woman. He might have lost his leg, but he hadn't lost his honor. 'Twas disrespectful and unchivalrous to...

The lass suddenly dropped the expensive spectacles to the floor and surged toward him. Before he could blink, she caught his face between her palms and planted a hard kiss square on his mouth.

What had possessed her, Alisoune didn't know. 'Twas quite unscientific. All she could fathom was that there was a prime specimen of a man standing within reach, that he was mysteriously attractive to her, and that something about the way he was regarding her made every nerve in her body quicken.

Her brain suddenly seemed to shut off, and she couldn't summon up a single intelligent thought.

Some other part of her took over then, thrusting her toward him, compelling her to try something she'd never experienced before—kissing a man.

The sensation proved to be rather pleasant. His mouth was firm, his skin warm, and he tasted faintly of apple.

She didn't consider whether he'd like it. And indeed, considering his lack of response, 'twas possible he did not. His mouth was immobile. He seemed to be holding his breath, though she was too mortified to open her eyes to check.

Now she was sure she'd done the wrong thing. Acting on impulse was seldom wise. But how could she extricate herself with grace?

Her fingers trembled where she touched his grizzled jaw, and she started to pull away.

Then she heard his crutch fall to the floor. In the next instant, his hands came up to caress her face. He tipped her head to the side. With a soft growl, he pressed his lips to hers and deepened the kiss. His warm breath sent shivers through her as he began to feast on her mouth like a beggar feasting on bread.

A bolt of current speared through her then, driving the intense pleasure he bestowed upon her lips down through her body, straight through her heart, deep into her belly, all the way to the vulnerable spot between her thighs.

She moaned at the curious heat building there as he kissed her with growing desperation. Her heart was

pumping hard. Her nerves felt on fire. A shimmering buzz encircled her head. Breathless with yearning, she returned his passion, opening her mouth and daring to explore him with her tongue.

He groaned, and for an instant, she imagined she'd hurt him somehow. But it must have been a groan of encouragement, for he swept one arm around her back to press her closer, crushing her breasts against him and letting his tongue tangle with hers.

Now the hot, tingling desire traveled slowly up from between her thighs to her abdomen, up through her belly to her breasts. Her nipples ached with exquisite need where they contacted his solid chest.

She wanted him even closer, though it seemed anatomically impossible. She weaved her fingers through his hair and drew his head down, arching up toward him at the same time, eager to be completely enclosed in his embrace.

But she miscalculated. She pulled too hard and began to fall backward. Though he staggered and thrust out his arm to try to keep upright, he lost his balance as well. Their mouths were torn apart, but she foolishly clung to him, not wanting to be separated from him for one moment.

Thankfully the bed was behind her. She landed with a painless plop on the feather mattress, and he twisted enough to wind up mostly off of her. The hound sat up and whined in concern, which made Alisoune giggle. But she wasn't about to let her own clumsiness interfere with this most enjoyable endeavor.

Giddy with delight, she wrapped her arms around the handsome man's neck, eager to continue, and smiled up at him.

But he wasn't smiling.

CHAPTER 4

Lachlan had never been so mortified in his life. This was the reason Margaret had left him, why he never let anyone close, why he wasn't deserving of a woman.

For God's sake, he couldn't even stand on his own two feet.

He'd utterly humiliated himself. He'd carried on like a lovesick cow, literally falling all over her, and now she was laughing at him.

She was right to laugh. He was a disgrace. He couldn't bring himself to look her in the eye.

"I'm sorry," he mumbled, shaking off her hands and trying to lever himself up off of the bed with as little ado as possible.

"Ye are?" She sounded hurt.

"I should never have…" he began, casting a glance over his shoulder for his fallen crutch. "'Twas a stupid mistake."

"'Twas?"

"Aye, and 'twill not happen again."

"'Twon't?"

"I'm…" He couldn't think of a better word to describe what a pathetic excuse for a man he was. "Sorry."

"Oh." There was an awkward moment of silence, and then she said, "Well…I don't think I am."

For an instant, his foolish heart fluttered. She sounded sincere. But that was just wishful thinking. Surely she was only being polite. Who wouldn't be sorry to be knocked over by a clumsy cripple?

He retrieved the crutch and got it under him, pushing back up onto his good leg. Though he tried to avert his gaze, his eyes couldn't help but be drawn to the breathless beauty sprawled on his bed like a fallen angel. Her green skirts were askew and puffed up like a dark storm cloud against the pale cream sky of his bed linens. Her long chestnut-colored hair had mostly come undone and swept her face in loose curls. Her eyes looked smoky now, like mist over a green sea. And her mouth was stained a luscious shade of crimson, darkened by the pressure of his kiss.

But 'twas pointless to admire her. He was only torturing himself. Clearing his throat, he withdrew and turned toward the hearth, grating out, "The porridge should be ready."

He set down the tip of his crutch, put weight on it, and heard an awful crunch.

He wouldn't curse in front of the lass. 'Twasn't seemly. But he longed to spit out a string of the foulest words he knew.

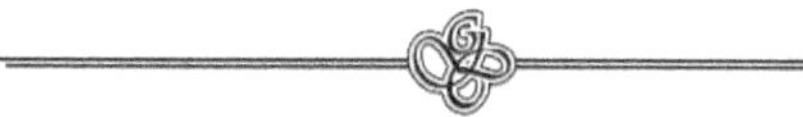

Her soft gasp as she saw her prize spectacles crushed beneath his crutch was like salt in his wounds. God's teeth! He was an arse, an idiot, a fool unfit for company, better off alone where he could do no harm.

He spoke through teeth clenched in shame. "I'll...find a way to repay ye. I'm sorry for..." He paused and let out a sigh of regret. "For everythin'."

"Nae!" she hastened to assure him as he continued to limp toward the fire. She wriggled down off the bed and followed him. "'Tisn't your fault. I'm the one who...who..."

He lifted the bail of the pot and gave her a brief sidelong glance. She was blushing.

"I shouldn't have kissed ye," she admitted, her hands clasped modestly before her. "But I'm not sorry. 'Twas a most... pleasurable experience, well worth the cost of a pair o' spectacles."

He closed his eyes. Surely she wasn't serious. She only felt sorry for him. 'Twas pity, not affection.

And yet...a part of him was stupid enough to hope she was telling the truth.

He opened his eyes again and lifted the pot from the hearth. He didn't speak while he filled two crockery bowls with the porridge.

She squeezed her clasped hands tightly together atop her stomacher and asked softly, "Are ye so angry with me then?"

He frowned, unable to figure out how she'd come to that conclusion. "Angry with ye?"

"For takin' liberties with ye."

He glanced up at her. Faith, she was serious. She

thought he was vexed with her for...for "taking liberties" with him? He bit back a smile. Taking liberties wasn't usually the sort of thing a woman did to a man.

She mistook his pause for condemnation. "Ye *are* angry." Her shoulders sank. "But ye must know, kind sir, I meant ye no harm. 'Tis only that I've never kissed a man before, and I have a curious nature, so I—"

"Never?" That was a surprise. She seemed awfully good at it for a novice.

She shook her head and pressed a hand to her bosom. "I didn't know what to expect. I didn't realize my heart would pound so fiercely...my blood would run so warm...my whole body would burn with such a heat that I could no longer think straight or—"

"I'm not angry," he blurted out before she could say something to drive him even more mad with longing.

She bit her lip then, effectively silenced. He slid the bowls to their respective places on the table. She located and replaced her own spectacles, and then collected the shards of the ones he'd broken and threw them into the fireplace.

He had only one chair. Spotting his dilemma, she scooted the table over to the bedside and sat atop the mattress, leaving the chair for him.

Fortunately, he had two spoons. He gave her one, kept one for himself, and eased down into the chair. Then he sat staring at his bowl of porridge.

He had no appetite. All of his hunger was focused between his legs. It had been months since the beast in his trews had stirred, but 'twas most definitely stirring

now. And now that 'twas awake and ravenous, there wasn't a damned thing he could do about it.

The lass spooned a generous mouthful of porridge into her mouth and closed her eyes in bliss. "Mmmm."

His groin tightened. He clenched his jaw, then stabbed his spoon into the porridge, shoveling it past his teeth.

"Mm-mm," she crooned.

He swallowed the porridge in one giant gulp. It sank to his gut like a stone.

"Mmmm." She licked her lips.

He gave her a pained expression. "Can ye not...that is...must ye..."

She looked at him with wide eyes, her spoon poised between the bowl and her delicious mouth. "Aye?"

He shook his head. 'Twas no use. The lass couldn't know what she was doing to his insides. He'd have to suffer in silence. Soon enough they'd be done eating, and he'd send her on her way.

Alisoune wasn't sure why he looked so miserable. Aye, she'd overstepped her welcome, grabbing him and kissing him like that. But it had been most rewarding...at least for her. Until she'd knocked the poor man over, he seemed to be relishing it as much as she.

She wondered if she could repair the damage she'd done. When men of science failed in their experiments, they usually scrapped everything and started over.

"Perhaps we could begin anew," she suggested. "Ye can forget my improper advances, and I'll forget the

broken spectacles." She stuck out her hand. "My name is Alisoune, Alisoune Hay."

He stared at her hand in surprise as if she'd placed a dead mouse on the table. She withdrew it. Maybe she was being too forward again.

He sighed, seemed to think it over, and then gave her a nod. "Alisoune," he repeated. She liked the way her name sounded in his deep, rolling voice. "I'm Lachlan."

"Sir Lachlan, happy to make your acquai—"

"Not Sir," he interrupted. "Just Lachlan."

She glanced again at his battle gear in the corner. She supposed if she'd lost her leg in a fight, she'd like to forget she'd ever been a knight as well. "Sorry."

"Nae," he said with an apologetic grimace. "'Tis fine. I just…I won't be donnin' armor again. I'm just Lachlan."

Eager to move away from an obviously uncomfortable subject, she quickly said, "The porridge is quite tasty."

He gave a single soft bark of amusement. "Porridge is porridge."

"Not at all," she countered. "Ye have to have the right proportion o' solids to liquids, the right distance from the heat source, and the right time of exposure to the heat."

"Is that so?" The soft twinkle in his silvery eyes let her know that he found her engaging, if a bit odd. But then everyone found her odd. At least he didn't seem to think she was Satan's spawn.

They both went back to eating. Finally Lachlan gestured toward her spectacles with his spoon. "Do those truly help ye see better?"

"Oh, aye," she said. "Without them, I'm as lost as a

lamb in a snowstorm. But with them…" She studied his face for something she could point out. "I can see the tiny white scar ye have at the corner o' your mouth there." She nodded to the mark.

He lifted his finger to touch the spot, as if he'd forgotten it.

"Impressive," he said. Then a roguish glimmer shimmered in his silver eyes. "Can ye see the whiskers on Campbell's chin?"

She whipped her head around toward the hound, who was sitting by the bed, licking his chops, waiting for scraps. "Aye."

"What about his eyelashes?"

She narrowed her eyes. "Aye, just barely."

"And what about that flea perched on the end o' his muzzle?"

She squinted for an instant before she realized he was jesting. Then she erupted into bubbling peals of laughter.

CHAPTER 5

Lachlan knew he'd carry the sweet sound of her laughing with him to his grave. It had been a long while since there had been any joy in his life. 'Twould be a long while before he was likely to have any. So he stored the lovely sound away in his memory, to pull out on days when loneliness and despair got the best of him.

Meanwhile, Alisoune was enticing his hound with the dregs of her porridge.

"Did ye hear what your master said about ye, Campbell? He as much as called ye a flea-ridden mongrel. Come on now, pup. I'll give ye a wee bit o' my porridge to soothe your injured pride."

The hound lapped her bowl clean and then eyed Lachlan's.

"I suppose ye'll be wantin' mine as well?" he said. "Ye've spoiled my hound, lass."

"Oh, I'll wager he was spoiled long ere I arrived."

She was right. As Lachlan's only companion, the trusty deerhound lived in relative luxury. Lachlan set his bowl on the floor, and Campbell made quick work of it.

Alisoune rose then and gathered their dishes.

"I can do that," he grumbled.

"O' course ye can." Nonetheless, she made herself at home, pouring water from his bucket into the empty porridge pot and hanging it to heat over the fire again.

'Twas admittedly convenient having her help. Lachlan had let the cottage go, mostly because there was no one worth keeping it clean for. But he didn't want her to think he was helpless. He got up from the table, took his cloak from its peg, and picked up the empty bucket.

Murmuring, "I'll be back," he lifted the latch of the door with his elbow and nudged it open. Campbell eagerly nosed outside, leaving the door wide, and Lachlan limped out after him through the snow, heading for the spring that coursed through the forest.

The day had turned gray and frigid, but not frigid enough to cool the residual passion that simmered in his veins. A part of him wished that he and Alisoune *could* start over and that she'd never kissed him. 'Twould be hard to forget the honeyed taste of her lips.

When he reached the spring, he leaned his crutch against a tree beside the icy water. Holding onto the trunk for balance, he lowered the bucket, filling it slowly. Then, with his crutch under one arm and the bucket in the other hand, he made his difficult way back to the cottage, careful not to spill too much.

The dog had relieved himself by then and nudged the

door open for him. But when Lachlan stepped with his snow-covered boot on the flagstones, it slid, and a lightning bolt of pain suddenly streaked down his missing leg. He caught himself on the crutch, but not before a wave of water slopped out onto the floor.

Embarrassed, he glared sharply at Alisoune. She was busy rinsing out the bowls and didn't seem to notice. The calf of his missing leg was throbbing now, which infuriated him. After all, it should be impossible to feel a limb that was no longer there. He hoped to God 'twasn't going to be one of those days that he spent clutching his stump in agony. Compressing his lips and ignoring the pain as best he could, he bent down to replace the bucket.

"Is it still cold out?" she asked without meeting his eyes.

"Aye," he said, hanging up his cloak.

"'Tis been an unusually frigid winter."

"Aye."

"It looks like another storm's comin' in, aye?"

"Maybe."

"So there'll be more snow."

He frowned. The pain in his leg was beginning to ease. "If a storm comes, I suppose so, aye."

"Ye'll be grateful for a big roarin' fire to sit by then."

Lachlan's brows converged. She wasn't just fascinated by the weather. Something else was on her mind.

He was fairly certain he knew what she was after. And he was just as certain he should deny her. After all, he'd already been more than generous. He'd hidden her from an

angry mob. He'd fed her breakfast. He owed her no more.

But though 'twas against his instincts, his better judgment, and his will, in the end, he knew he couldn't refuse the lass.

Alisoune didn't want to ask Lachlan outright to let her stay. But she feared the stubborn soldier was never going to ask her himself. And if he didn't, she didn't know what would become of her.

If she returned to her room at the inn in Keirfield, 'twould only be a matter of time before the priest dragged her out of it and finished what he'd started. If she left, she'd not only be leaving behind all of her possessions—her coin, her clothing, her tools—but she'd likely be caught without a cloak in a winter storm before she could reach her home in Stirling.

Then again, why should Lachlan invite her to stay? He was perfectly content as he was. For the moment at least, he had a roof over his head, a warm fire, and a faithful dog.

Besides, she'd doubtless annoyed him by breaking into his house and forcing her affections on him. And she'd probably bored him with Copernicus's theory and her collection of spectacles.

'Twas no use. She'd never convince Lachlan 'twas to his benefit to harbor an outlaw. She wouldn't blame him if he tossed her out on her heretical arse.

He prodded the coals on the fire and let out a lungful of air. "If ye're wonderin' whether I'm goin' to turn ye over to the villagers or out into the snow, ye needn't

fret. Ye're welcome to stay...till the storm passes."

Relief welled in her heart as she said, "Oh, thank ye, sir. Ye won't be sorry. I...I'll make your meals and fetch your water and make sure your hound—"

"I don't need your help," he said rather defensively.

"Oh, I'm certain ye don't," she said carefully, though 'twas plain his cottage needed a thorough scrubbing from top to bottom. "But I don't have much coin left, and I can't stay here in all good conscience without earnin' my keep."

Before he could have second thoughts about letting her stay, she grabbed a rag and began wiping down his cupboards.

Meanwhile, he made up the bed with one hand, cut a generous piece of salted meat for Campbell from the slab hanging in the kitchen, and put another log on the fire.

"Ye know, I have to admire the way ye get about on one leg," she told him as she scrubbed at the porridge pot. "I mean, everythin' must be a challenge...walkin'...fetchin' water...carryin' wood. But ye don't seem to let your adversity stop ye."

"I don't have a choice."

"Well, a lesser man might give up." She pushed her spectacles up on her nose. "How long has it been since ye lost it?"

She had the feeling, from the grim look in his eyes, that he could probably tell her down to the minute. Instead, he mumbled, "About three months."

"Is that all?" She turned to stare at him in wonder. "And ye've adjusted that well already. Can ye still feel it?" Alisoune was admittedly intrigued by the concept of

phantom pain. She'd never talked to anyone with a missing limb before. 'Twas the perfect opportunity to do some firsthand scientific inquiry.

"Nae," he grunted.

Her face fell. "Truly? Because I've heard that—"

"Ye can't believe everythin' ye hear."

"Nae, I suppose not."

Still, when she glanced at him hobbling toward the hearth, she could tell by the subtle tightening around his mouth that he did indeed feel some sort of pain. 'Twas just like a soldier to try to deny it.

She wondered if there was any ease for him, if there was any way to eliminate or diminish his suffering. She was in the habit of looking for solutions. 'Twas the bane, she supposed, of possessing a scientific mind.

But she also genuinely wanted to help the man. He seemed lonely and uncared for, living alone in this wee cottage far from town. By the melancholy cast of his eyes as he gazed into the fire and the deep lines etched into his forehead, it had been a long while since he'd had a happy thought or a kind word or a good laugh. Perhaps it had been a long while since he'd had reason to laugh.

She might not know yet how to ease his physical pain, but she thought she could probably coax a chuckle out of him.

She set aside the clean pot, and then returned to the bed and began riffling through her satchel.

"Come here, Campbell," she called. The dog obediently ambled over and sat before her. She pulled out her box of spectacles and found the biggest pair. Campbell was very

patient. He sat quietly while she strategically perched the oversized spectacles on his nose.

"What do ye think, Lachlan?"

What Lachlan was thinking as he gazed absently into the fire was that he should never have told Alisoune his name. It sounded too enticing upon her lips. He was already having trouble keeping his mind off of the bright ray of sunshine who was, much to his chagrin and against his wishes, lighting up his cottage and warming his heart. But when she said his name…

He reluctantly lifted his eyes. What he saw made his face crack into a grin. His buffoon of a deerhound looked like a wise old scholar.

"Oh! Wait," Alisoune said, digging in her satchel. She nudged Campbell around to face her and tied a white coif around his head. To Lachlan's amazement, the dog put up with her machinations without moving a muscle. She tied a red ribbon around the dog's neck and sat back to admire her handiwork.

"There," she said, turning the hound toward him. "Laird Lachlan, Lady Campbell wishes to make your acquaintance."

A snort of laughter escaped him. The dog made the ugliest woman he'd ever seen.

She pretended to politely introduce the hound. "Lady Campbell, Laird Lachlan."

Lachlan shook his head. "Ach, Campbell, have ye no shame?"

"Shame?" Alisoune cried, affecting great affront. "Why, Laird Lachlan, Lady Campbell takes great offense at that. Don't ye, Lady Campbell?"

Campbell lifted his muzzle and gave a mournful howl, and Alisoune broke out in infectious giggles. Lachlan couldn't help but join in. And the more they laughed, the more Campbell howled, until the cottage was filled with a loud and eerie mix of misery and merriment.

Eventually, the dog shook off the annoying accoutrements and slunk off to sit at the hearth, sulking in humiliation.

Alisoune was still hiccoughing when she removed her spectacles to wipe her eyes.

Lachlan's belly was sore from laughing. How long had it been since he'd laughed, truly laughed? Half a year? More? It felt good, like flexing his sword arm after a long absence from the battlefield.

He was still smiling when she put her spectacles back on and flashed him a wide, radiant grin. He realized now that her beauty didn't come from her appearance. She was beautiful by virtue of her honest face, her kind soul, and her sweet nature.

There seemed to be no artifice in her. What she appeared to be, she was. What she said, she believed. 'Twould be a lucky man who laid claim to a lass so pure of heart.

That last thought dimmed his happiness. He would never be that man. Nae, a woman like Alisoune deserved a whole man—a man who could care for her, love her...protect her.

CHAPTER 6

For Alisoune, there was nothing quite as satisfying as finding the solution to a problem. 'Twas the reason she enjoyed selling spectacles. Choosing the correct lens and instantly improving a person's sight was gratifying.

But that wasn't the only reason Alisoune's heart swelled at her success in coaxing a laugh out of Lachlan.

The way his teeth flashed, the silver sparkle in his eyes, and the easy chuckles that started low in his chest gave her a glimpse of the man Lachlan used to be...before misfortune befell him. That man was kind and fun-loving, mischievous and merry. And Alisoune thought she liked that man very much...very much indeed.

She caught her lip under her teeth. Of course he clearly didn't feel that way about her, which wasn't surprising. Alisoune made most men uncomfortable. Not only was she odd-looking—tall and spindly and bespectacled—but she was also too clever and outspoken

for her own good. Men were intimidated by her, which was why, of course, the good folk of Keirfield wanted to burn her at the stake.

Still, Lachlan hadn't wanted to burn her at the stake. And aside from the unfortunate kiss she'd forced upon him, he didn't seem to feel threatened by her.

She glanced over at him. He stood by the window now, peering out the shutters. His face had gone grim again, as gloomy and gray as the weather.

She bit her lip. 'Twould be a challenge, luring him out of whatever pit of despair he'd fallen into, lifting his spirits and returning him to the carefree man he'd been.

But Alisoune loved challenges. They taxed her scientific brain. If she could solve Lachlan's problems, if she could choose a lens for him that would make him see his world and his life with new clarity, 'twould be rewarding indeed.

She'd start by clearing out the cobwebs, literally. His cottage was sadly neglected, much like the man himself. Perhaps if he could see restoration in his living quarters, 'twould give him hope for himself. Smiling in determination, she snatched up the broom and set about sweeping the corners of the ceiling to dislodge the spiders.

Then, because she found it difficult to be silent with all the interesting thoughts constantly whirling through her brain, she began to muse aloud.

"A spider web—that's it!" she exclaimed, staring up at a heavily webbed beam. "Can ye see, Lachlan? Our galaxy is like a gigantic spider web. And we've been thinkin' all

along that we're the great spider in the midst o' the web, that the other planets are like flies caught in the strands. But what if 'tisn't true? What if the *Sun* is the great spider, and we're one o' the flies?"

She glanced at Lachlan from the corner of her eye. Would he mock her as most men did? Or would he simply stare at her as if she were daft?

He did neither. He listened and frowned and seemed to consider her idea. "But how can that be? I can see the Sun goin' from east to west, circlin' around us."

"True! However..." She thrust aside the broom and sought out objects to illustrate her point, finally settling on one of his apples and a small round stone she found on the mantel. "What if 'tis only a difference in perception?" She held up the apple. "Say this is the Sun. 'Tis circlin' the Earth here, aye?" She moved the apple slowly around the stone.

He nodded.

"But what if 'tis reversed? What if the Earth is circlin' round the Sun?" She held the apple still and circled the stone in the opposite direction around the apple. "To our eyes, 'twould appear the same, aye?"

His brow furrowed, but a spark of enlightenment glittered in his eyes. "Hmm."

"'Tis the heliocentric hypothesis!" she said in triumph, replacing the apple in the bowl.

He scratched at his beard. "Is this why the priest thinks ye're a witch?"

"Well," she admitted, rolling the small stone between her palms, "men o' the church don't much like men o'

science. It upsets them a great deal to have their doctrine questioned."

"No doubt."

"But ye don't think I'm a witch, do ye?"

"Nae." He reached down to scratch his hound's ears. "Campbell doesn't let witches in the house."

She smiled, tossing the stone up a few inches and catching it.

"Ye'd better be careful with the Earth there," he warned her.

She giggled, then cocked her head at the round stone in her hand. 'Twas most unusual. "Where did ye get this?"

He smirked. "From a witch."

Scolding him with a dubious glance, she held the stone up to the light. It looked like polished crystal, but it had curious cracks in the interior that made milky filaments in the stone.

"A strange old crone brought it to me in the middle o' the night," he explained. "She called it the Winter Stone. She said 'twas a magic relic that could change a man's fate."

"Magic? I don't believe in magic." She examined the crystal closer. It shimmered in a rainbow of hues as she rotated it slowly from left to right, confirming her suspicions.

"It seems to change color," he said. "I'm not sure about changin' a man's fate."

"If this is what I think 'tis, it might indeed change your fate. It looks like a rainbow crystal. The cracks inside create an internal prism, which refracts the light into various

colors. Stones like this are very rare and quite valuable."

He snorted. "Then why would she give it away?"

The instant Alisoune looked up at him, an eerie tingling arose at the back of Lachlan's neck, stirring his memory.

Dark hair.

Bright green eyes.

Take the Stone to its rightful Keeper.

Could it be? Could Alisoune be the Keeper the old crone was raving on about? But how could she have known? After all, the lass hadn't arrived at his cottage till hours after the old woman disappeared.

Lachlan wasn't sure he believed in magic either. But 'twas hard to explain the events of the past day using reason.

"I think she meant it for *ye*," he said.

"Me? Pah!" She set the stone carefully back on the mantel. "Nae, ye should hold onto it. No doubt 'twill fetch a king's ransom."

A king's ransom. What would he do with a king's ransom? Coin meant nothing to him, not when he had no one to share it with. He'd gladly give up a king's ransom if he could only get his brothers back.

But that wasn't what the old crone meant by changing his fate. And he was sure the lass must be the one the crone intended to have the crystal. He wasn't normally superstitious, but he'd told the old woman he'd deliver the relic to its Keeper. Just to be safe, before Alisoune left, he'd tuck the stone into her satchel.

She continued to clean his cottage, wiping the counters, tidying up the food stores, sweeping the floor. While it pleased him to see his hovel being restored to order, it also made him feel guilty for having let it become so filthy.

He tensed his jaw. He felt as if he should stop her. Not only was it not her duty to look after him, but 'twas not something he needed. Why should he live in a nice home anyway while his brothers dwelt under the cold, hard, blood-soaked ground of Haddon Rig?

He narrowed his eyes at the sunny lass in the green gown, who was humming to herself as she swept the ashes from in front of the hearth. She was far too sweet to suffer his bitterness. He might want her to stop, but he didn't have the heart to disappoint her by refusing what she deemed a good deed.

"I'm goin' out for a while," he said, buckling on his belt and slipping his dagger into its sheath.

"Oh?"

He owed her no explanation. But she deserved one. "I'm takin' Campbell for a hunt."

She smiled and pushed the glasses back up on her nose. "Be sure to be back ere the storm starts."

"I will."

"And dress warm."

"Aye." He'd already pulled a floppy woolen cap down over his head.

"As for ye, beast," she added, bending forward to address the hound, "bring us back a nice fat rabbit, and make sure your master doesn't lose his way in the woods."

Lachlan shook his head as he grabbed his cloak. Lose his way? Alisoune sounded like a worrisome wife.

He shrugged on the cloak and opened the door. 'Twasn't yet snowing, but 'twould be soon. Campbell bolted out past him, and Lachlan hesitated in the doorway, giving her a meaningful look. "Be sure to latch the door shut after me."

Alisoune did so immediately. She doubted the priest would come after her again today, not after Lachlan's threat. But 'twas probably wise to err on the side of caution.

Meanwhile, she would see what she could do to make his home more accommodating.

She pried open the wooden shutters over the only window in the cottage and polished the dingy diamond-shaped panes until they were transparent again. She weeded good food from bad, throwing handfuls of hopelessly shriveled vegetables onto the fire. She chipped the wax from candles that had dripped onto the floor and used it to polish the two oak chests near the foot of his bed.

In one of the chests, she found clean bed linens, so she stripped off the old. She tightened the ropes beneath his mattress, which she managed to flip over with some effort, and then made up the bed with fresh linens. She fluffed his feather bolster until 'twas light and airy and spread his snowy sheepskin coverlet over the top.

After an hour of sweeping, scrubbing, and sorting, the

cottage began to look livable. Now 'twas time to make it comfortable.

Mopping her brow with the back of her arm, she scanned the interior, imagining what 'twas like for Lachlan, managing with only one leg. She decided that the most difficult thing was probably getting out of bed on his crutch. What would be useful was a bracing mechanism of some sort, some kind of rail he could use to pull himself up, something strong attached to the wall.

Fortunately, tidying his house, she'd found all sorts of odds and ends—tools, scraps, bits of wood and metal and leather, rope, nails—everything she'd need to make modest alterations to his living quarters.

Giddy with excitement over this small alteration and how 'twould improve his quality of life, she located the perfect spot for the bracket, the vertical wooden beam near the head of his bed. She was scouring the room, considering what she might use for the bracket, when her gaze lit on the armor he said he no longer needed.

CHAPTER 7

Campbell had been in fine form today, Lachlan thought as he patted the dog's head and slung the third rabbit over his shoulder. 'Twas as if the dog knew they had an extra mouth to feed.

He glanced up at the sky. Heavy gray clouds had gathered now, blotting out the heavens and lying atop the pines like a thick sheepskin. The air was cold and still. The snowstorm would arrive soon.

He winced as he leaned heavily on his crutch. His leg, his *missing* leg, was burning again. No matter how many times he told himself 'twas impossible—one couldn't feel pain in a missing limb—his missing limb couldn't be convinced of that fact.

He wondered if the lass was right. He wondered if nerves *were* like the roots of a tree. He wondered if a tree felt pain when one of its roots was lopped off.

Then he chuckled to himself. With all this wondering, he was beginning to sound like the lass herself.

She certainly was a curious woman, asking questions about missing limbs and spider webs and the universe. He'd never met anyone quite like her. 'Twas no wonder the priest thought her a witch.

From across the clearing, he spotted the cottage, and for an awful instant, he feared the worst, for there was no smoke coming from his chimney. Had the townsfolk come after all? Had they taken Alisoune?

Then he heard a loud banging from inside, and he caught his breath. She was apparently still there, though God only knew what she was doing. What she *wasn't* doing was keeping the fire going.

He stamped his boots on the threshold and rapped on the door.

"Who is it?" he heard her call from inside.

"Lachlan."

"Do ye have a rabbit?" she called back. "Because if ye haven't got a rabbit, I'm not lettin' ye in."

Lachlan couldn't help but grin at the saucy lass. "Suit yourself then. Campbell and I will build a fire and feast out here."

She unlatched the door and swung it open. He thought he remembered how she looked, but memory didn't serve him. After trudging through the dull snow under a wintry sky for the past few hours, looking at her was like having a first glimpse of spring in all its warm and verdant glory. Behind her spectacles, her eyes danced. Her smile was dazzling. And her laughter was as clear and musical as a babbling May brook.

The fire had dwindled to red coals, but he could see

she'd been busy while he was gone. In fact, seeing what she'd done to his cottage—the clean-swept flagstones, the tidy shelves, the freshly made bed—made his throat close with gratitude.

And yet it also quietly vexed him. What gave her the right to come into the life he was resigned to and try to change it? Why give him false hope?

Swiftly, before he could blurt out something he'd regret, something that would fill her beautiful green eyes with tears, he limped across the cottage and tossed the rabbits onto the table.

"Three?" she said, cheering. "Campbell, ye've done yourself proud!"

In a rare show of impertinence, the hound reared back on his hind legs and placed his front paws on Alisoune's shoulders, almost bowling her over. He licked her face, knocking her spectacles askew.

Not bothered in the least by the hound's familiarity, she grabbed his whiskered face and scrubbed behind his ears. "Aye, that's a good lad! Ye've earned your keep today, haven't ye?"

"Campbell, down!" Lachlan barked, just in case she wasn't as pleased as she sounded.

The dog instantly obeyed and Lachlan sent him to the hearth with a nod of his head.

Alisoune straightened her spectacles and immediately set to dressing the rabbits.

"I can do that," he said.

"Don't be silly," she countered. "Ye brought home the rabbits. 'Tis only fair I should prepare them." Then she

gave him a curious glance. "Ye must be weary. Why don't ye take a wee nap while I'm makin' supper?"

"A wee nap?" He scowled, and his words came out harsher than he intended. "I'm not an invalid. I'm just a man missin' a leg."

She smiled shyly and went back to work.

Meanwhile, Lachlan silently cursed himself. Why had he snapped at the lass? 'Twas obvious she was trying to help. He hadn't seen his cottage so clean since the day Margaret left him. Alisoune was kind to his dog, and she was civil to him. He had no right to speak to her so rudely.

"I'm sorry," he mumbled. "I'm not used to...kindness."

'Twas one of the saddest things Alisoune had ever heard. How could anyone be unkind to a person who was obviously suffering already?

But she'd quickly learned that Lachlan didn't like pity, so she kept her tone light. "Ye'll want to taste my rabbit stew ere ye decide 'tis kindness."

He chuckled once.

"Ye *can* help me by fetchin' the big pot," she said. If he wouldn't lie down on his bed, perhaps he'd notice the device she'd made for him when he drew near the fireplace.

But though he stood right beside the beam where she'd nailed the metal bracket when he bent to fetch the pot, he didn't seem to notice it.

"And the fire could use more fuel," she suggested.

She cut the rabbits into pieces while he stacked more wood atop the blaze. Still he didn't see the apparatus.

She smeared a lump of butter onto the bottom of the pot. Then she broke a few eggs into one bowl and a bit of flour into another, dredging the pieces and dropping them into the pot. She peeled and chopped an onion and an apple and added them with pepper and a few dried herbs from the cupboard. Then she lifted the heavy pot and handed it to him to hang over the fire.

Still he took no notice of the device.

While the rabbit sizzled away, filling the cottage with a delicious aroma that made Campbell lick his chops, Alisoune tried again to draw Lachlan's attention to her handiwork.

"The stew isn't burnin', is it?"

He peered into the pot. "Nae."

"Are ye sure ye won't sit down for a bit?" she tried. "Ye've been on foot for hours."

"I'm used to it."

She wondered. Even on two legs, trudging through something with the surface resistance of snow wasn't easy. "Even Campbell's worn out. Look at him."

Lachlan did look at him...and nothing else. When Campbell lifted his head, it wasn't six inches away from the bracket. But the man saw nothing. 'Twas incredible.

"I hope ye don't mind," she said, carefully ladling water into the pot and scraping up the cooked bits with a great iron spoon. "I tidied up a few things while ye were gone."

"Aye, I see." But nae, he did not see. He gave the room a cursory glance, no more. "Thank ye."

'Twas almost comical that he didn't notice what she'd done. She decided to let it go. Sooner or later he'd discover it.

While she tended to supper, he kept himself busy, bringing in a few more logs from his dwindling cache outside and scraping the rabbit pelts clean to use later.

They dined on the stew, which had turned out to be edible enough, despite a dearth of the usual seasonings Alisoune liked to use—saffron, cinnamon, and ginger. Perhaps such spices weren't as easy to obtain outside of large towns like Stirling.

She made sure Campbell got his fair share, despite Lachlan's grumbling protest that he'd rather have a third serving than waste such good food on a dog.

'Twas while she was cleaning up the dishes that Lachlan finally lowered himself onto to his bed and began to take off his boot. She pressed her lips together, trying not to smile in anticipation.

"What the devil?" he muttered. "What's my targe handle doin' on the wall?"

She spun around, beaming. "Isn't it grand? It should fit ye perfectly, because...well, the shield was designed to fit *your* arm, o' course."

He looked puzzled and, if she wasn't mistaken, none too happy. "Why is my targe handle nailed to the wall?" he repeated.

"Oh." She smiled sheepishly and rolled her eyes. "I should have said. 'Tis a bracket...for balance."

His brows came together.

Her smile faltered.

"A bracket?" He seemed upset.

"Aye." She took a few tentative steps forward, intending to show him how it worked. "When ye need to get out o' bed," she said, cautiously sidling past when he didn't move his knee out of the way and sitting beside him, "ye just grab hold like this..." She demonstrated. "And ye pull yourself up."

Some dark, fierce emotion raged in his silver eyes. She felt uneasy, the way she had when the priest and his followers had suddenly turned on her.

"My targe handle?" Lachlan's voice broke. That targe had served him in half a dozen battles and saved him in the last. He couldn't believe the lass had...had dismantled it.

"Ye said..." Alisoune's voice was a tenuous whisper. "That is...ye told me...ye didn't need your armor...didn't ye?"

Lachlan closed his mouth into a grim line. Aye, that was what he'd said. And 'twas true. What use did a one-legged soldier have for a suit of armor or a shield or a blade? 'Twas ridiculous.

And yet a small part of him had clung to the absurd belief that somehow he'd awaken from all that had happened as if from a dream, that he *would* fight another day, that he *would* go back to the man he once was.

"I'll put it back to rights if ye like," Alisoune said softly.

"Nae," he decided. She was right. He'd told her he was no longer a soldier. He just needed to accept that fact himself. A broken-down, war-wounded hermit had no need for weapons.

"'Tis no bother," she murmured. "I can change it back as fast as—"

"Nae," he said, forcing a fleeting smile. "'Tis fine. Thank ye."

He could see she was disappointed. She'd gone to a lot of effort, working the rivets loose from the targe and securing the handle to the beam at just the right height for him to pull himself out of bed. He had to admit, *'twas* rather ingenious.

But it also drew attention to the fact that he was different, that he couldn't function like a normal man. Hell, there was a time when he could have hopped up out of a lass's bed before her father even started up the stairs. Those days were gone.

Perhaps he was well rid of them. 'Twas time he accepted who he was, what he was.

"'Tis more than fine," he assured her, willing the warm sunshine to return to her eyes. "'Tis brilliant."

She blushed, but managed a tiny smile as she gazed down at him.

"Let's see how it works," he said, reaching for the handle to try it.

"O' course," she gushed, stepping out of the way.

A strange shiver passed through him as he took the familiar handle in his grip. He realized he hadn't done so since he'd come home from battle. A flood of unpleasant

memories abruptly assailed him, and his palm began to sweat around the iron handle.

But Alisoune waited expectantly, her hands clasped beneath her chin, a hopeful smile on her face. And Lachlan wouldn't disappoint her further. He refused to be debilitated by dead memories that couldn't be changed.

Slipping the crutch beneath his other arm, he pulled himself up by the handle.

Where before he'd strained the muscles of his good leg to stand up, only to hastily and painfully catch himself under the arm with the crutch, now he rose with ease, assisted by the strength of his arm. Where he usually dipped and swayed, trying not to fall, now he simply held onto the bracket until he was balanced.

He looked down at Alisoune in wonder. 'Twas such a simple device, such a humble gesture. But it made all the difference in the world. Gratitude made a thick lump in his throat as she smiled sweetly up at him.

Damn, he wasn't going to weep, was he?

Willing his tears away, he let the crutch fall back onto the bed, reached out his free hand to lift Alisoune's chin, and placed a chaste kiss of thanks upon her smooth brow.

At least it started out chaste.

But Alisoune apparently had her own ideas about what a kiss should be, now that she was an expert on the subject. She slipped her fingers into his hair, stood on tiptoe, closed her eyes, and pressed her mouth against his with all the passion of a long-lost lover.

CHAPTER 8

Alisoune had feared Lachlan would never kiss her again. She'd been wanting him to for hours now. Of course she'd told him they could start over and pretend it had never happened. But that wasn't what she truly wanted. She'd only said that to be polite.

This breathtaking intimacy and the delicate yet powerful surge of desire that rose in her when their lips touched was too delicious a forbidden fruit to be denied.

There was no turning back now, no pretending it hadn't happened. As her mouth moved softly over his, she sighed. If she'd known how enjoyable kissing a man was, she'd have started long ago. Now she intended to make up for lost time.

And this time she didn't have to worry about taking liberties. After all, *he'd* started it.

His hand cupped the back of her head, tilting it slightly, and his fingers stroked beneath her loose braid as he deepened the kiss. She felt his hot, rapid breath

upon her cheek, tasted the intoxicating ambrosia of warm apples and sweet desire in her mouth.

She melted against him, relishing the way his long hair brushed her face and his supple leather doublet pressed upon her breasts. This time, instead of forcing him off-balance, he relied on the bracket to keep him upright.

'Twas fascinating, the current that sizzled through her veins from the simple act of kissing him. She was well-versed in most of the sciences, but when it came to the science of courtship, her knowledge was a vacuum. Would the current intensify if she grew more bold? Would she overheat? How much more could she endure?

Eager to find out, she drew closer, running her hands down his throat and across his chest, and then sliding them around his waist to the small of his back.

He groaned low in his throat, and the sound sent a frisson of primal longing through her that lodged with a jolt betwixt her thighs. Answering with a soft moan of her own, she slipped her hands slowly down until they cupped his buttocks. She squeezed gently, and through his trews, she felt his muscles flex.

Then she felt something extraordinary. Where her belly contacted his, he began to swell, hardening, pressing against her with tangible need.

The primitive nature of such a response triggered her own desires, launching them to new heights, and she found herself aching to...to...

Lachlan tore his mouth free, even as his body cursed him

for it. He withdrew his hand from her and hung his head, gripping the bracket with white knuckles and panting heavily from the rush of lust that had almost made him lose his mind.

Not since he'd lost his leg had his loins stirred like that. In truth, he hadn't been sure 'twas still possible. But there he was, straight as a lance and hard as a rock.

Yet to what end? Alisoune was not the sort of lass to be trifled with. She was a young thing, an innocent. He wouldn't take advantage of her inexperience for his own selfish ends.

When he hazarded a glance at her, 'twas almost too much to bear. The combination of desire and confusion in her eyes was alluring and heartbreaking all at once.

"Did I...do somethin' wrong?" she asked breathlessly.

A rueful chuckle escaped him. "Nae, lass."

"Then why...?"

How could he explain?

"Come," he said, lowering himself to the bed and patting the space beside him. "Sit."

She did, but when her gaze wandered with wicked interest to his groin, he tossed the sheepskin coverlet over his lap.

"Ye said ye'd never kissed a man before, aye?"

"Aye." Then she turned to him in concern. "Did I not do it properly?"

He smiled in spite of himself. "Oh, aye, ye did it properly." He scratched his beard, wondering how to proceed. "Ye just did it with the wrong man."

"What do ye mean?"

"Ye need to save your affections for the man ye mean to marry."

She furrowed her brows. "What if I don't mean to marry?"

"Not marry?" he scoffed. "A bonnie lass like ye? Half o' Scotland's bachelors must be knockin' at your door."

"Pah!" She blushed and swatted his arm. "And what about ye? Would ye be knockin' at my door?"

The corner of his mouth quirked up. Ordinarily he wouldn't have thought he could be attracted to such an odd, clever, scrawny mouse of a woman. But there was something about her—her charm, her wit, her sincerity—that did indeed draw him to her.

Still, she couldn't possibly be drawn to him.

Instead of answering her, he said, "'Tis easy to mistake lust for love." He felt as if he spoke for his own benefit as well. "'Tis only the heat o' the moment that's turned your head."

She gave him a dubious stare, then considered his words. "So ye think 'tis pure science? Basic alchemy?"

Nae, he didn't think that at all. But perhaps 'twas best to agree with her. "Aye, most likely."

"Hmm."

She didn't look pleased with that idea, but at least the heavy-lidded desire was fading from her face. Now if only 'twould fade from him as well...

Alisoune felt dissatisfied and disappointed. It seemed she'd been on the cusp of some important discovery, so

close to the truth. Then, abruptly, all her theories were dashed.

She still felt an ache deep within her body, still felt the residue of current sparking in her veins. Was he right? Could the way she felt have nothing to do with rational thought or deep emotions, but rather be caused by a simple mixture of elements, an alchemy for passion?

She didn't think so. She might not be as experienced as he was when it came to kissing. But she'd been around men before. She'd never particularly wanted to kiss any of them, not like she did Lachlan. There was something different about the way he made her feel, something she didn't think could be explained away by science.

But she supposed 'twas pointless to think about it now. His mind was clearly elsewhere.

Lachlan had let Campbell out one last time for the evening and banked the fire. As ridiculous as 'twas, he refused to let her sleep by the hearth, insisting she take his bed. He'd listen to no amount of arguing, claiming that his chivalry would keep him warm. So she reluctantly acquiesced, leaving him to stretch out on the floor.

Still feeling unsettled, Alisoune took a long while to fall asleep, finally drifting off to the sounds of Campbell's snoring.

It seemed she'd only just closed her eyes when she heard a rasping sound in the dark. She frowned and lifted her head a few inches to hear better.

'Twas Lachlan. He was talking in his sleep. The sound was faint and incoherent. He must be dreaming.

She pushed up onto her elbows, getting her bearings in the dim firelight. Campbell was still snoring. The dog was probably accustomed to his master's nocturnal conversations.

But Lachlan's voice began to grow more and more urgent, and soon his breathing quickened. He suddenly flailed out an arm, startling her.

She bolted upright. She could see he'd dislodged the cloak he'd draped over himself. Now he lay gasping and twitching on the flagstones.

With a soft cry of worry, she scrambled out of the bed and rushed to him.

"Lachlan," she called gently.

His eyes were still closed tightly as his head rocked back and forth.

"Lachlan!" She touched his brow.

Campbell was awake now. He shot to his feet and trotted over, sniffing his master in concern.

Lachlan jerked and emitted a sleep-muffled scream.

Her eyes wide, Alisoune shook him by the shoulder. "Lachlan!"

But still he would not awaken, and he was shuddering as if with sickness. On instinct, she knelt down, wrapped her arms around him, and held him close.

Almost at once, he calmed. The furrow left his brow, his breathing slowed, and he relaxed back into the oblivion of slumber.

As she cradled him, giving him comfort, she wondered what horrible dream he'd had to affect him so. She suspected he dreamed of battle. Most soldiers did. She'd

heard that some were never the same after they'd gone to war, that nightmares haunted them the rest of their lives. Was that true of Lachlan?

Campbell seemed to answer her as he sadly lowered his head and returned to curl up in his spot by the fireplace.

She meant to return to the bed after Lachlan fell asleep. Somehow she didn't make it.

Drifting slowly awake, Lachlan felt a warm, womanly body curled up against him, and he smiled. There was nothing like having his bonnie Margaret welcome him home from war.

His eyes still closed and a wicked grin on his face, he snuggled closer, teasing her soft, round bottom with his swelling dirk.

Then his smile faded. His brow creased. That was a memory from another time. That was before…

His eyes flew open, and he pulled back at once, waking her. Not Margaret. Alisoune.

"Aristotle's beard," she exclaimed sleepily. "How did I get here?" She stretched out both arms, yawned, and then turned to him with a smile.

Of course she *would* smile first thing in the morning. What else did he expect? The lass was sunshine personified.

"Oh, I remember now," she said, rising up on her elbows, which made her square neckline dip low on one shoulder. "Ye were havin' a nightmare."

He frowned. He didn't remember. He never remembered his dreams.

What he *did* remember in all-too-vivid detail was the way she'd felt nestled against him a moment ago. He might have imagined she was Margaret, but to the lusty beast in his trews, a woman was a woman. That part of him was still as hard as steel and expecting to be pleased.

The fact that Alisoune was only inches away, her hair sleep-mussed, her eyes softly sparkling, her gown threatening to fall off of her any moment now, didn't help matters.

"I should split more wood for the fire," he announced under his breath. Maybe hard labor and the bracing cold would extinguish the fire in his loins.

Was that disappointment he glimpsed in her eyes?

It didn't matter. She'd be leaving soon anyway. The storm would clear, and there'd be no reason for her to stay. Besides, he thought with black humor, if she left, he wouldn't need to trouble himself with taking a bath.

Aye, 'twas for the best, he decided as he began the difficult task of levering himself up from the floor.

"Here, let me help ye." She jumped up.

"Nae!" he growled, half in ire, half in shame. "I can do it myself." At her crestfallen expression, he added more gently, "I've managed alone so far. I'll have to manage alone when ye're gone."

If the words caught unexpectedly in his throat, and his eyes grew moist, 'twas probably just ash from the fireplace. That happened when you slept next to a fire.

As soon as he was up, he threw on his cloak, whistled

to Campbell, and headed outside with his hand ax to split what little wood he had left. He'd have to fetch more before the day was done.

Lachlan's words haunted Alisoune. *I'll have to manage alone when ye're gone.* Of course he would. But it saddened her to think of leaving. And 'twas disappointing to think that her brief time with him would change nothing, that he'd forget her as readily as one forgot a squirrel scampering through the yard.

She wanted to help him somehow, to make his life better. She didn't want him to slowly let the cottage return to its former squalor. She couldn't bear to think of him moping in lonely exile.

She'd made that bedside bracket for him, which had pleased him enough to earn her a kiss. Was there anything else she could do for him?

Outside, she could hear him splitting logs as she poured oats and water into the porridge pot. His supply of wood was almost gone. He'd need more soon. She would have offered to collect wood for him, but she knew he'd refuse. He seemed determined to prove he could manage by himself.

Chopping wood must be extraordinarily difficult for him. Not only would it be hard to manage an ax while standing on one leg, but he'd have to make a number of trips into the forest to get enough wood to last even one day, since he could only bring back what he could carry over one shoulder.

She pushed the spectacles higher on her nose and tapped on her lip. She wondered...

Campbell was big and strong. And he had *four* legs. If she could construct a sled of some sort with a harness for the big deerhound, he could probably haul a good deal of wood.

Setting aside the pot, she scanned the room for something that could serve as a sled. Her gaze stopped on Lachlan's battle-scarred steel breastplate. That would slide easily across the snow and, later, across the grass. She could fashion a yoke and harness out of wood and leather and attach it to the breastplate with rope.

Giddy at the prospect, she whirled just as Lachlan came in the door. "Lachlan, I need to borrow Campbell."

"Borrow him? What for?"

"I..." She glanced at the half-empty bucket. "I need to fetch more water."

"Give me a moment," he said, placing chunks of wood on the coals. "I'll fetch it for ye."

"Ach, nae...ye...nae," she said, stumbling over her words. "I...I could actually do with...with a breath o' fresh air." She may have overdone it by fanning herself. "'Tis terribly hot in here."

He frowned at her as if he thought she were mad. She couldn't blame him. 'Twas a bumbling excuse. "I can open the door and—"

"Nae! Nae, nae, nae, ye don't have to..." She sighed. "To be perfectly honest...I..." She could think of no plausible reason to leave the cottage.

He asked quietly, "Do ye need to attend to...women's matters?"

"Aye, that's it," she said, beaming. "I need to attend to women's matters, aye. And...Campbell..."

"Will keep ye safe."

"Exactly." She grinned, grateful he'd supplied the perfect, if vague, excuse for her.

While he kindled the fire, she secretly stuffed some rope, wood, and leather scraps into her satchel. Then she swirled on her cloak, and, when his back was turned, concealed his great armored breastplate underneath it, staggering out the door under its weight with Campbell at her heels.

The snow was falling lightly now, and she found to her delight that the breastplate made quite an excellent sled. With Campbell frolicking beside her, she dragged it all the way to the edge of the woods and a spot shielded from snow by thick pines where she could work.

Campbell was patient while she fitted him with the yoke, as if he understood he was taking on an important responsibility. Once she had his harness in place, she attached it to the breastplate with two lengths of rope so 'twould drag behind him.

Then, because she couldn't resist the temptation, she had Campbell take her for a wee sled ride across the snow. There was only one mishap when he started too quickly and she took a tumble off the back of the conveyance.

By the time she returned to the cottage, smoke was curling up from the chimney, she was dusted with snow

and flushed with pleasure, and Campbell's entire body was wagging with joy.

"Now don't say a word, Campbell," she whispered to the dog. "'Twill be a surprise."

She unfastened the yoke and sled and propped them against the wall where the stack of wood had been. Then, looking as casual as possible, the two conspirators entered the cabin to enjoy a steaming breakfast of porridge.

CHAPTER 9

"Somethin' is up with ye two."

Lachlan was sure of it. He might not know the lass well enough to read her expressions, but Campbell's guilt was written all over his face.

"Why do ye say that?" Alisoune asked with wide-eyed innocence, spooning more porridge into her mouth.

"Because Campbell looks like he's been eatin' kittens."

She giggled, almost losing her porridge.

He clucked his tongue. He supposed he'd find out eventually what the two of them were up to. In the meantime, he tried to enjoy his porridge. 'Twas nigh impossible when his attention kept drifting to the rosy-cheeked lass, who this morning looked as rare and beautiful as a rose in winter.

He still couldn't believe she'd slept beside him last night on the cold flagstone floor. The softhearted lass had sacrificed her own comfort to comfort him.

No one had done that for him before. His nightmares

had always frightened Margaret. 'Twas one of the reasons she'd left him.

He never recalled the dreams. But when he woke in a cold sweat, breathing heavily, crushed by a vague sense of despair, 'twasn't hard to guess what he'd been dreaming about.

To realize that this lass he hardly knew, who'd crossed his path by chance, might wish to understand his pain...

He swallowed his last bite of porridge and looked up at her through suddenly watery eyes.

How could he bear to have her leave?

Yet how could he be so cruel as to wish she'd stay?

She smiled back fondly, warming him instantly and making him feel like she'd known and loved him all his life.

He cleared his throat and pushed himself up on his crutch, turning away. "I've got to go...fetch more wood."

"Now?" she asked, springing to her feet.

Keeping his eyes averted, he shrugged on his cloak, pulled on his cap, and muttered, "Better now, before the snow's heavy."

"Well then," she said cheerfully, "Campbell has somethin' he'd like to show ye."

Here 'twas—whatever they'd been up to. He supposed he wasn't going to be able to make his escape just yet. He wiped his nose with the back of his sleeve and said with false cheer, "Does he?"

"Come on, Campbell," she sang out. "Show your master what a handy beast ye are."

The hound came to attention and began yipping excitedly, something he rarely did. When Alisoune opened the door, Campbell charged out, bounding crazily in the snow and snapping at snowflakes.

Befuddled, Lachlan shook his head. "What did ye feed my dog to make him so wild?"

She winked at him. "Kittens."

He smirked.

She called Campbell back to her and began attaching some sort of leather harness over the dog's shoulders. When Lachlan saw her drag his breastplate—his fine polished steel breastplate with the Lion of Scotland engraved on it—across the ground to secure it behind the hound, his jaw clenched. But he managed to hold his tongue.

And then all at once he understood.

"'Tis a sled." He laughed in delighted wonder. "To transport firewood."

She nodded vigorously, joining in his laughter.

He was amazed, truly amazed. "But how did...where did...what...?"

He grinned down at her. She smiled up at him. Then she closed her eyes and lifted her face, clearly expecting a kiss of thanks.

He gulped. He didn't dare kiss her. 'Twouldn't be fair to her. 'Twouldn't be fair to either of them. There was no future in a kiss between them. 'Twould only be a taste of something they couldn't have.

So as much as he longed to press his lips to hers, and as much as he knew it hurt her when he didn't, he turned

away and feigned a sudden keen interest in Campbell's new conveyance.

Alisoune opened her eyes, and then frowned in discouragement. If she didn't know better, she'd think Lachlan didn't care for kissing. But his body certainly responded to it. So why did he deny himself what was so pleasurable?

'Twas only a wee kiss, after all.

Aye, she understood what he'd said about saving herself for her husband. She wasn't a fool. She knew that men preferred their brides to be unbedded. But at the moment they were nowhere near a bed.

She sighed in resignation and wrapped her cloak tighter about her, trying to take joy in the way Lachlan was experimenting with his new toy.

"Come on, lad," he called to Campbell after he'd dropped his ax into the sled. "Let's try out this new device."

He waved his hand and gave her a lopsided grin of gratitude before he set off with Campbell toward the woods, disappearing in the quiet fall of snowflakes.

At least she'd managed to coax a smile from him, she thought, if not a kiss.

He was gone for a long while. Alisoune cleaned up breakfast and straightened the bed linens. She washed her face and hands and rinsed her teeth. She even took out her disheveled braid, combed her hair, and replaited it. But still he didn't return.

Bored, she began investigating the cottage more thoroughly.

He had a small store of spices, and she uncorked each of the tiny vials and sniffed at them, identifying them by name.

The trunk at the foot of his bed was unlocked, and she dug through his clothing, which was mostly linen shirts, woolen trews, and one rich black velvet doublet, for special occasions, she supposed.

She more closely examined each piece of armor, forgetting that he must have been wearing it when he lost his leg, shocked by the dark bloodstains that peppered the dull steel and by the notable absence of one of his greaves.

Then, because for Alisoune, curiosity always outweighed horror, she began to wonder, since the greave was missing, what had become of the leg inside it. Had he left it on the battlefield? Had he buried it? Had he brought it home for Campbell to gnaw on?

Silently scolding herself for such irreverent and grotesque thoughts, she put the armor back where she found it and picked up the round crystal on the mantel.

'Twas a beautiful thing. She'd never actually seen a rainbow crystal before, and she discovered that as she rolled it back and forth between her fingers in the firelight, it did seem to shine in different colors. At the moment 'twas a bright green, but when she turned it in just the right way, it flashed violet.

What had Lachlan said—that the stone was meant for

her? Why would he think that? After all, she'd only appeared in his cottage yesterday.

Still, it felt soothing in her hand, the perfect size, almost as if 'twere made for her palm. It shimmered blue as she replaced it.

Then, impatient, she decided to keep a vigil at the door. Lachlan had told her to latch it, but she was sure nobody would bother coming for her in this weather. After all, 'twas nigh impossible to burn a person at the stake while snow fell to extinguish the flame.

Besides, she thought as she swung open the door, ushering in a cloud of snowflakes, she'd just come up with another way to make the dour Lachlan laugh.

Lachlan's spirits hadn't felt so light in a long time. The sled worked perfectly. 'Twas just as well she'd made it from his breastplate, since he had no other use for it. And even Campbell seemed proud to be of service. With the hound's help, he was able to chop and stack enough wood to last several days.

He wondered why he hadn't thought of such a brilliant solution. He supposed, wallowing in his misfortune and distracted by grief, it had been difficult to think of anything else.

Alisoune, on the other hand, had proved herself a genius. She'd immediately ferreted out his need, designed an effective remedy, and produced it. This one wee change in his life would make a great difference.

He'd never met a woman like Alisoune. Hell, he'd never met a *man* like her.

As he limped home, with Campbell dragging the sled by his side, he thought maybe the crone had been right. This lass, this Keeper of the Stone, was indeed a special individual. And it seemed, whether the stone had anything to do with it, Lachlan's life *had* been changed, just as the old woman predicted.

He was almost home, less than a dozen yards from the door of the cottage, when an object suddenly flew past his shoulder. He ducked aside, and then turned to look for it. Had it been a bird? A rock? Behind him was only snow.

He turned back in the direction from which it had flown, and at that instant, a second object hit him full in the face.

'Twas cold and hard, and it stung where it hit him. He wiped wet snow from his face with the back of his hand and tried to see who was assailing him.

So stunned was he to see a grinning Alisoune launching another projectile at him that he had no time to duck out of the way of the third snowball, which struck him with deadly accuracy. His cap flew off from the impact, and he almost lost his crutch.

"What the devil!" he shouted, brushing bits of ice from his eyebrows.

She laughed and lobbed another hard-packed snowball at his belly.

He turned sideways, but not swiftly enough to avoid taking a hard impact to his arm. He swore, but his grin belied his anger.

"Is it war then?" he called out.

She answered with another snowball that glanced off his hip.

"Ach!" His appetite for revenge was whetted now, and he muttered under his breath, grinning all the while, "We'll see about that, lassie."

She'd stacked up an enormous store of munitions. The lass was likely to pummel him soundly before he managed to pack a single snowball. But surely his aim was better than hers.

While he rapidly compressed snow between his palms, she threw two more frosty missiles. One hit his neck, sending shivers of ice down his shirt. The other impacted harmlessly on his crutch.

"A-ha!" he gloated, rearing back his arm and hurling his snowball forward.

But the little minx was ready for him. She'd appropriated his targe. She fended off the blow with a glance of his shield, then fired her next missile over the top of it.

Clearly he was going to lose this battle. And Campbell was of absolutely no use. The hound, his mind still on his serious wood-hauling duties, took no interest in their foolish play.

Alisoune was laughing triumphantly now, firing snowballs as if she were storming a castle, while he only managed to land one feeble clump of snow that struck the top of her head, dislodging her spectacles and showering flakes down over her face and shoulders.

She squealed with the cold shock, and he grinned in victory.

But her recovery was quick. With a shake of her head that scattered snowflakes everywhere, she reseated her spectacles, and then picked up a hefty missile in each hand and threw them in rapid succession.

Somehow he managed to duck *into* both of them and ended up with white splotches on the side of his doublet and the front of his trews, which sent her into gales of laughter.

He'd never win this lopsided battle, he decided, if he played fair.

CHAPTER 10

Alisoune hadn't had so much fun in years. Not only was she enjoying the thrill of competition, but the challenge of calculating the most effective angle of trajectory kept her brain entertained as well. So far, she'd landed her strikes with impressive accuracy.

She hurled another snowball at him, which hit him smack in the middle of the chest. But this time the blow made him stagger backwards, and his crutch slipped out from under him. As she watched in growing dismay, his arms cartwheeled, and he lost his balance. To her horror, he fell back, hard, into the snowbank, where he lay...silent.

Her jaw fell open. "Lachlan?"

He failed to respond. She dropped the second snowball from limp fingers.

"Lachlan?"

There was no answer. She stared at him in dread, gathering her skirts in clenched fists.

"Lachlan!"

She stumbled toward him, whimpering in fear under her breath. What had she done? Was he hurt? Was he dead? What ever had made her think 'twas a good idea to pummel a crippled man with snowballs?

He still hadn't stirred when she reached him. He lay sprawled and motionless on the snow, like a beautiful dark angel fallen to earth.

"Oh, Lachlan," she breathed in fright, clapping her hand over her mouth.

But she couldn't let panic distract her from reason. Steeling her nerves, she rushed forward and knelt by his side, using her fingers to feel for the pulse in his neck.

To her great relief, his heart was still beating. But he wasn't awake. She furrowed her brow in worry. She'd heard that after a blow to the head, sometimes people could dwell in a state of deep sleep for days. They eventually wasted away, never regaining consciousness.

"Oh, Lachlan," she said in despair, shaking him gently. "I only meant to cheer ye. I didn't mean to hurt ye."

She bit her lip. If he didn't waken straightaway, she'd have to get him inside so he wouldn't freeze. But how? He must outweigh her by half.

She glanced back over her shoulder at Campbell. Perhaps she could unload the wood and use the sled to transport him.

While she was considering the best course of action, and before she could move a muscle, Lachlan rose up, grabbed her, and rolled her onto her back in the snowbank.

She gasped in surprise and relief. "Ye're awake!" But a closer look into his twinkling eyes told her the truth. "Ptolemy's ballocks! Ye played me false."

Pinning her by the shoulders, he grinned down at her like a wildcat with a mouse between its paws.

"Ach!" she spat. "Let me up!" The snow was cold on her backside.

"Only if ye'll cede the battle."

She was vexed with him. After all, he'd scared the hell out of her, and she'd been worried. But when she beheld the merry sparkle in his silver eyes and the flash of his snow-white smile, she couldn't stay angry.

She shivered. "'Tis cold, Lachlan! Let me up!"

"Oh, I *know* 'tis cold. I was lyin' there for quite a while myself."

"Ye brute!" she cried, grinning in spite of herself. "Let me go!"

"Do ye yield?"

"Ye cheated!"

"Ye gave me no choice." He shook his head and clucked his tongue. "What sort o' villain attacks a helpless cripple anyway?"

"Ye're not helpless, ye big oaf!"

"Now ye're callin' me names." He sighed in mock disgust. "'Tis appallin'."

She laughed and pounded on his chest, but he didn't budge.

"*And* beatin' me."

She tossed her head, throwing off her spectacles. "Campbell!"

He laughed. "The dog's not goin' to help ye, lass. Come on now, ye've lost the fight. Surrender."

"Never," she mumbled under her breath.

He cocked his head. "What was that ye said? I didn't quite—"

"Never!" she said, laughing.

"As ye wish." He shrugged. "I've no place to go. 'Tisn't my arse freezin' in a snowbank."

She gasped, then giggled.

The wet snow was indeed seeping into her skirts. But as she continued to gaze up into Lachlan's dancing eyes, 'twasn't long before she no longer felt the cold.

Lachlan watched Alisoune melt before his eyes like snow in sunlight. He knew that look. The lass was all hot and hungry again.

And this time—curse his male instincts—so was he.

When her eyes drifted languidly down to his parted mouth, he was so drunk on his joy and her laughter that he didn't hesitate or even think before kissing her.

She tasted as fresh and clean as the fallen snow. As she gasped against his lips, the light fog of her breath moistened his face. Her fingertips were icy as she touched his cheek, but her kiss warmed his blood so thoroughly that he hardly felt the cold.

Her body was soft and welcoming beneath him, and to his astonishment, he fell into her embrace as easily as laying his head on his own familiar pillow.

Her shoulders were bared by the wide square

neckline of her stomacher, and he stroked her tenderly there with his thumbs. She moaned softly and arched up, inviting his caress with her pale bosom.

He obliged her, running one knuckle along the upper edge of her gown and delving beneath with his finger. Her skin was supple and impossibly smooth, like fine silk, and he sighed into her mouth with pleasure.

But she wanted more. She threaded chill fingers through the curls at the back of his head and drew him down toward her, then slipped her mouth aside and offered him her throat.

With a low knowing chuckle, he kissed her delicate jaw and then lower, making a burning trail beneath her ear and down the side of her neck till she shivered at the sensation.

His own body, meanwhile, had gone instantly rigid with desire. It wanted only one thing. And the more he kissed her lips, her throat, the upper curve of her breast, the more intense his longing grew.

She arched even more, as if commanding him to touch her where she willed.

He knew what she was asking for, even if she didn't. With a broad stroke of his tongue, he grazed her bosom, nuzzling aside the fabric of her white linen chemise to taste her sweet flesh.

Her hands made fists in his hair, and she squeezed her eyes closed in bittersweet yearning, turning her head aside to grant him access.

He gently tugged her stomacher down to reveal the pale perfection of her small breasts.

She drew in a shuddering breath and held it in anticipation. With a seductive smile, he teased one of them with the tip of his tongue and then, when she gave a little cry of need, enclosed her fully in his mouth.

He was sure there could be no greater heaven than this. She tasted like smooth honey mead on his tongue, mellow and spicy and intoxicating. And when he drank his fill and moved to her other breast, she dug her fingers into his back with ill-concealed lust.

He'd thought his body had forgotten how to respond to a woman. But he was wrong. He ached with yearning and thickened with purpose.

She squirmed beneath him, and he remembered she was lying on the frozen ground, probably soaking her skirts with snow. Kissing his way back up to her other ear, he reached a hand beneath the curve of her hips and lifted her, rolling onto his back with her so that he would bear the brunt of the ice.

Her cheeks as she gazed down at him were flushed with cold, but a raging fire burned in her eyes. That look alone made his blood surge, and he groaned with desire.

The impetuous lass attacked him then, raining kisses over his face and throat and the vee of his chest as if to sample every inch of his flesh. With breathless enthusiasm, she wrenched open the buttons of his doublet, and her hands slipped beneath his linen shirt, gliding over his shoulders, across his chest, and along his ribs.

It felt divine. For so long he'd been bereft of touch,

bereft of affection. That Alisoune would give herself so freely and lovingly to him was akin to setting a banquet before a starving man.

He felt like laughing with delight as she boldly explored him. And then she pressed a brazen palm against the front of his trews, and the laughter stuck in his throat.

He sucked a breath through his teeth and closed his eyes in delicious agony. But just as the curious lass began to loosen the laces of his trews, he heard Campbell growl.

Biting back a curse at the interruption and careful not to alert Alisoune, Lachlan peered through narrowed lids to see what troubled the hound. Then his eyes widened.

In the distance, a dark figure stood, watching them. At Campbell's second warning growl, the man turned in a huff and lurched off in the direction of the village, his black cloak stark against the white snow.

The man was too far away for Lachlan to identify. But whoever 'twas had probably recognized Lachlan and would babble to all of Keirfield what he'd seen.

Lachlan didn't care a whit what the townspeople thought of him. But he had to protect Alisoune. Already, the lass had pricked the pride of Father Ninian. If that infernal priest heard that she'd been seen sporting with Lachlan in the snow...

As difficult as 'twas to end such a pleasurable endeavor, Lachlan forced himself to gently seize Alisoune's wrist, stopping her passionate pursuit. He

retrieved his cap and her spectacles and whispered, "Let's go inside, lass."

Father Ninian's secretary, fleeing purposefully toward Keirfield, was so overwrought with religious zeal and righteous fervor that he could hardly scramble fast enough through the snow. He pursed his thin lips in disgust. The father would hear about this.

He'd seen Lachlan Mar fornicating with the witch. He was sure of it. They'd been copulating shamelessly, right there in the snow, in plain sight of God...and everyone else, for that matter.

He licked his lips. 'Twould be a long while before he could scrub from his memory the sight of the crippled soldier fondling the spectacle-seller's undersized teats.

Mar probably wasn't to blame, he decided. 'Twas probably the fault of that scheming witch. She'd probably ensorceled the poor wretch.

After all, the soldier had kept mostly to himself after he lost his leg and his Margaret. He didn't go to church. He didn't strike up conversations. He only came to town for supplies. He wasn't the sort of man to carry on with a strange woman.

Besides, he was a cripple. God had punished him. He clearly wasn't meant to enjoy such worldly diversions. 'Twas sinful that a man with one leg should be encouraged to partake of pleasures he didn't deserve, of what rightfully belonged to pious men whom God had seen fit to bless with whole bodies.

Father Ninian was right. The lass was the handmaiden of the devil, and Mar was wrong to try to protect her from the fires of purification.

He didn't wish to be seen as too overeager. But he couldn't wait to tell Father Ninian what he'd witnessed.

By the time Lachlan unhitched Campbell, unloaded the sled, stacked the wood, and hung up his cloak, Alisoune realized his lusty mood had faded. He'd doubtless had enough time to reconsider their impulsive actions and he felt guilty now. He was stoking the fire on the hearth, but the fire in his heart no longer burned brightly. He seemed...distracted.

What he didn't realize was that she had no intention of giving up so easily. She'd never been intimate with a man before. The way Lachlan made her feel, she was positive she was on the verge of some soul-shattering discovery. And she meant to pursue it. Alisoune was nothing if not persistent. She could be as pesky as a flea.

Determined to seize the day, she loosened the laces of her stomacher and, leaving only her linen chemise, casually drew her gown over her head, ostensibly to dry it by the fire.

Though he said nothing, his eyes coursed over her with an obvious flicker of appreciation, and she saw his breath catch.

She draped the gown over the back of the chair near the fire. Then she turned to warm her own damp

backside, strategically placing herself between Lachlan and the fire, where the light of the flames would silhouette her body.

He tried to ignore her...and failed. Guilt might be a powerful force, she decided, but 'twas no match for lust. His fist clenched on his crutch, and his jaw tightened as he stared intently past her and into the flames.

"I'm goin' to town," he finally muttered.

She raised her brows in surprise. "Ye are? Now? Why?"

"I have to...get some...supplies."

He wasn't a very good liar. Perhaps she'd been too seductive and was scaring him off. She crossed an arm over her bosom, self-conscious now. "When will ye...be back?"

"I won't be long."

His face was grim. He didn't meet her eyes as he shouldered his satchel and tied a pouch of coins onto his belt. The familiar jingle alerted Campbell, who jumped up to his feet, ready to accompany his master.

"Campbell," he commanded, "stay."

The dog reluctantly sank back down onto the floor.

"Latch the door," he reminded her, nodding briefly in farewell.

She gave him a timid smile. But inside, her heart was sinking.

CHAPTER 11

Alisoune stared in silence at the closed door for a full minute before latching it and then turning dejectedly towards the fire. Atop the mantel, the curious white stone caught her eye as it reflected the leaping flames, and she idly picked it up.

What had she done wrong? Why had he fled? In the snow, everything had seemed perfect. What had happened?

She cupped the stone in her palm, gazing down at it as if the answer lay there while a dozen possibilities raced through her brain.

She'd been too forward.

She hadn't been forward enough.

She was too tall, too awkward, too thin. Too smart.

He didn't like lasses with spectacles.

He didn't like lasses who made a spectacle of themselves.

As she looked down at the stone in her hand, it

seemed dull now, just an ugly lump of worthless rock. Alisoune felt like that, ugly and worthless.

Sighing, she reached up to replace the crystal, but it slipped from her fingers and dropped with a hard smack onto the floor, and then rolled across the flagstones.

She gasped. What if she'd cracked it?

Campbell got to it before she could, bringing the stone back to her. She took it gently from between his teeth and examined it. Fortunately, 'twas unbroken. The only flaw in the stone were the cracks inside, which of course were what made it so unique and interesting.

As she gazed down at the crystal, she couldn't help but smile at the parallel. Wasn't that true of people as well? Wasn't it a person's flaws that made them unique and interesting?

The way the stone lay cradled in her hand now, it appeared to glow in a beautiful rosy color. Her thoughts likewise began to take on a more rosy cast.

'Twas true that most men seemed to feel threatened by Alisoune's flaws. They were uneasy around her. But Lachlan was different. He didn't mock her or shun her or think she was Lucifer's progeny.

He must have fled for some other reason. She furrowed her brows and rolled the stone between her hands.

Then, all at once, it came to her.

Lachlan might feel the same insecurities she did. He was also flawed—physically and mentally scarred. He might figure he was cursed by God, undeserving of kindness, not entitled to compassion or pleasure or love. Maybe that was why he had panicked and left.

With a lightened heart and renewed spirits, Alisoune carefully placed the crystal back on the mantel, where it flashed bright green before wobbling to a stop.

She knew what to do now. She'd send Lachlan such a strong message of acceptance and caring and affection that he'd *have* to believe it. Indeed, a brilliant idea was already forming in her head.

"How about if we go for a wee walk, eh, Campbell?" She grinned as the dog's tail began to wag. "Would ye like to show me where the spring is?"

Lachlan didn't know which was worse as he limped home through the snow—his pain or his anger. Damn it, there was no godly reason he should feel such agony in his toes. They weren't there any longer.

What had Alisoune called it? Phantom pain. Well, if *'twas* phantom pain, he was a desperately haunted man.

At least he'd taken care of that meddling busybody who'd been spying on them. One glance at the black-cloaked secretary's ruddy cheeks and heaving chest, and Lachlan knew he had his man.

He hadn't needed to say much. Lachlan's size spoke well enough for him. But he *did* advise the squirming weasel as he held him by the throat that if he valued his continued good health, he should forget whatever he'd seen and stay away from Lachlan's cottage.

Satisfied he'd put the fear of God into the man and knowing Alisoune was safe enough with Campbell to guard her, he'd taken time to stop by the grocer to

purchase a few onions, eggs, preserved figs, a bottle of sack, and, on an extravagant whim, a small box of sugared almonds.

The last time he'd made the trip into the village, there had been no snow. On one leg, it had taken him a long while. But this time 'twas a tortuous ordeal as he balanced the satchel of goods over his shoulder and battled through thick snowdrifts. Halfway home, the cursed pain returned with a vengeance.

'Twas a reasonable price to pay, he supposed, for surviving the battle, for living when his brothers died. Still he had to fight the urge to stop where he stood and lie down in the snow until either it passed or he froze solid.

But he had to get home. He had to get back to Alisoune. He may have cowed the secretary for now, but Lachlan was no fool. He realized that time had a way of dulling a man's fear.

By the time the cottage was in sight, he was grimacing at every step. Walking had made the ache worse, and he despaired of ever being without pain again.

At least he had Alisoune to look forward to—Alisoune with her sweet smile and gentle touch, her compassionate nature and her amusing antics. Indeed, her latest antic—the one where she'd oh-so-innocently stripped to her chemise, leaving herself nearly naked to his view—almost made him forget his pain.

Several agonizing minutes later, he finally reached the cottage. He brushed the snow from his shoulders and knocked at the door. Once it opened, he was greeted by

Campbell's wet nose...and struck by the bitter realization that when Alisoune left, Campbell would be the only friend to ever greet him at the door.

His attempt to appear cheerful didn't fool her for an instant.

"What's wrong?" she said in concern, rushing forward to take the satchel from him. "Ye're so pale." She brushed his forehead with her thumb. "And ye're drippin' wet."

Her words made a lump form in his throat. The lass was fawning over him. Nobody fawned over him anymore. "I'm fine," he croaked.

"'Tis your leg, isn't it?" she guessed. "Ambroise Paré has a theory that when a nerve is severed, it becomes more sensitive to the cold." He had no idea who Ambroise Paré was, but he let her take his icy hand in her warm one just the same. "Come. I think I have just the thing for ye."

She drew him slowly forward. He glanced past her. There by the fire was his giant wooden tub, generously filled with water.

He blinked. How had she managed to fill it? That much water would take hours to transport. "How did...?"

She grinned smugly and nodded to another device she'd assembled while he was gone.

"'Tis a water transport. It fits over Campbell's yoke," she explained. "He can carry two evenly balanced buckets o' water now. Between his two buckets and my two, it took only three trips to the spring to fill the bath."

Words failed him. 'Twas another ingenious invention. The lass had given him a gift beyond value. He'd have no

reason to scrimp on water now. He could take a bath every day if he so chose.

"Ye thought o' this yourself?" he marveled, hanging up his cloak and combing a hand back through his hair. "I hardly know what to say."

She smiled. "Ye don't need to say a thing."

She began ladled boiling water from the pot over the fire into the cold water of the tub to warm it.

"What ye *do* need, however," she added, "is to get out o' those damp clothes."

He hesitated. Until he'd met Margaret, who cringed at the sight of a naked man, he'd never been particularly shy about his male anatomy. But that wasn't what gave him pause now. He was wary of letting Alisoune see the mangled stump of his leg.

She mistook his hesitation for modesty. "Ye needn't fret," she assured him. "I'll just take off my spectacles." She plucked them from her nose and tucked them into the front of her stomacher. "There. Now I'm as blind as an owl in daylight."

Mollified by her claim, he undressed. For Lachlan, standing stark naked in front of a beautiful lass, whether or not she could see him, had an immediate and dramatic effect. He was glad her sight was impaired, for if she'd looked at him now, she'd have seen that more than just his leg had become a shocking stump.

Alisoune suppressed a smile. Owls weren't actually blind in daylight, and neither was she. 'Twas only a myth. But

Lachlan didn't know that. And she wasn't about to tell him.

Instead, she surreptitiously savored every delicious inch of him as he eased his magnificent body into the water.

She hadn't exactly fibbed. Her vision wasn't ideal. Things in the distance blurred into unrecognizable shapes. But when she was close to an object, or in this case a handsome man, her sight was only slightly impaired.

Indeed, 'twas good enough that the vision of his broad chest and wide shoulders emerging from the steaming water took her breath away. His body was covered in muscle, and he looked as brawny as a bull. He could have crushed her with his powerful arms, though at present, they were draped with leisurely abandon over the edge of the tub.

He closed his eyes and let out a long, blissful sigh. She was glad to see the warm water was doing its work. It had broken her heart to see him looking so pale and troubled.

She didn't want to get her gown wet, so she stripped down to her linen chemise. Then she pretended to guide her way with her toes along the flagstones, groping aimlessly as she settled onto her knees beside him.

Wetting the spicy-scented soap, she casually peered down into the water. But the clever knave adjusted his seat in the tub just then to lean forward, obstructing her view.

He cleared his throat. "If ye'll give me the soap, I can—"

"Do it yourself? Oh, nae, 'tis no trouble, no trouble at all. 'Tis the least I can do after ye walked all that way for... What did ye get anyway?"

She moved behind him, out of his reach, ere he could snatch the soap—and the pleasure of bathing him—from her.

"Onions. Figs. Eggs. A bottle o' sack. Oh...and sugared almonds."

"Ooh, sugared almonds," she cooed, adding coyly, "and do ye intend to share them?"

He shrugged. "Oh, I don't know. Campbell doesn't much like sugared almonds."

She scoffed and lightly thumped the back of his head. "Naughty rascal."

Then she wet the soap and began to scrub patiently at his scalp, humming softly and occasionally peeking over his shoulder to see if she could catch a glimpse of...anything. But the way his knee was bent, his broad thigh blocked her gaze.

She finished his hair, rinsing it with clean warm water, and then moved down to soap his back. His muscles rippled under her fingers, and their lean, sleek suppleness did something to her insides, making her heart race. Suddenly she wanted to sample *all* of his textures.

When she slid the soap up over his shoulder, her wicked fingers let it go. It slipped down his chest into the water with a plop.

'Twas only natural her hand should follow.

He sucked in a quick breath when she reached for it.

But what else was she to do? She couldn't very well bathe him without the soap.

And of course, he should realize that without her spectacles, 'twould take a while to find it. She took her time looking, searching every delicious nook and cranny, apologizing when she happened to graze a sensitive spot.

"Ah, there 'tis," she said at last, finding it nestled against his lean buttock.

He emitted a shuddering sigh, and she resumed bathing him. She ran the soap down his massive arms, marveling at his strength. She weaved her fingers between his to wash them, enjoying the way they fit together.

'Twas when she moved to his legs that he tensed.

She paused. "Is the warm water not helpin' your pain?"

"Aye."

She resumed bathing him, soaping his good thigh and knee and calf. But when she moved to the other leg, he seized her wrist to stop her.

"What is it?" she asked.

His mouth worked as if he struggled to find the right words. "'Tisn't a fit sight for a softhearted lass."

"But I told ye I'm as blind as—"

"I don't believe owls are all that blind," he chided. "And I think ye know it."

She caught her lip beneath her teeth, aware she was blushing and unable to do anything about it.

He continued. "Just give me the soap and I'll—"

"Nae," she countered, pulling free of his grip. "I'm not

some fainthearted, lily-livered maid to swoon over a man's limb."

"Ye've never seen a limb like this."

"A limb is a limb."

"'Tisn't a limb. 'Tis a stump."

"A stump then."

"An ugly, misshapen knob o' flesh that—"

"Oh, for the love o' Pythagoras!" she said in amused exasperation, rolling her eyes. "Give me your damned leg ere the water gets cold."

CHAPTER 12

Lachlan would rather bare his arse than his ugly stump. 'Twas something he kept hidden, something he didn't want anyone to see, especially not a woman he...

What? Cared for? He dismissed the thought at once. 'Twas foolish to go down a road that went nowhere.

He supposed he was being overly defensive. But he didn't want to see the affection in her eyes dimmed by horror.

Then again, why not? She was leaving anyway. What difference did it make whether she left in tearful apology as Margaret had or ran screaming from the cottage?

"Fine." With a resigned sigh, he leaned his head back against the edge of the tub and closed his eyes to slits.

Alisoune wasted no time, delving both hands into the water and lifting his thigh with all the reverence of a bear hauling a trout from the stream. He braced for her grimace of revulsion.

But it never came. Instead, she began studying him intently, turning her head this way and that, even donning her spectacles to inspect every horrifying scar and twisted sinew, all without so much as a wince of disgust.

"Remarkable," she murmured. "Does it still hurt?"

"A bit."

"Not as badly?"

"Nae."

"'Tis the heat o' the water," she said triumphantly. "Paré was right."

He wondered if he should send Paré a gift of some sort. 'Twas strange, but the more Alisoune studied his mangled leg, the less awkward he felt.

"Do me a favor," she requested, her eyes sparkling, "in the name o' science. Close your eyes, and tell me where ye feel my touch."

He looked at her skeptically, but saw no harm in humoring her. He closed his eyes.

She ran her palm down his thigh, rounding the spot above his knee where his leg had been severed. A sudden twinge coursed down his shin and into his toes. His eye twitched.

"Where do ye feel that?"

He didn't want to tell her.

"Lachlan?" she urged.

He sighed. "I feel it in my damned toes."

"What about this?"

He felt a soft pressure under his missing heel. He shook his head. "My heel."

"And this?"

He felt the whole bottom of his missing foot, but it didn't hurt or tingle or burn. It actually felt improved. He opened his eyes.

She was rubbing and pressing at the end of his thigh. "Better?"

He nodded.

"Aha!" She grinned. "Ye see? If your nerves can fool your brain into thinkin' your leg hurts, then you can fool your brain into thinkin' ye're relievin' the pain as well."

'Twas amazing. Not only did her touch ease his pain, but it eased his fears. She didn't find the sight of him abhorrent at all. She found him fascinating...almost as fascinating as he found her.

As Alisoune resumed bathing him, her delight at having made an important scientific discovery began to pale in the light of a newer, more interesting revelation.

Lachlan was watching her. His eyes had softened, and his silvery gaze roamed over her. She felt it on her hair, on her lips, along the neckline of her chemise. He must have appreciated what he saw, for when she chanced to lower her regard, she could clearly see his ready response beneath the water.

The sight of him had a curious effect on her. Her nether regions began to ache, and her breasts tingled, remembering the sweet caress of his tongue. The more she touched him, the more aroused she became, until she craved something more than just bathing him.

Using her fingers, she combed the clean, wet hair back from his face. Then, on impulse, she caught his face between her hands and leaned forward to give him a quick kiss.

But 'twasn't quick at all. He replied with a kiss of his own, lifting his wet fingers to tangle in her hair and tilting her head to a more desirable angle.

She closed her eyes, dissolving into his embrace. So compelling was his kiss that she forgot about everything else. The outside world disappeared. All that existed were their lips, entwined in glorious counterpoint.

Her braid dipped into the bath, but she didn't notice. The sleeves of her chemise dragged through the water, but she didn't care. She was barely aware, when he wrapped his arms around her, pulling her closer, that she half-fell, half-climbed into the tub atop him.

With only her thin, drenched chemise between them, she could feel every inch of his muscular, bath-warmed body against hers. His hands slipped down her neck, along her shoulders, and then lower, to caress her breasts through the wet linen.

She gasped into his mouth, and he answered her with a bold stroke of his tongue. He moved one hand lower still, over her chemise, past her belly, as their tongues engaged in a lustful feast.

And then he found the spot where her need was centered. The instant he pressed his fingers between her thighs, intense pleasure zagged through her like a lightning bolt.

She groaned and moved against him instinctively.

Heat flashed through her body, and her heart raced. Her breathing grew shallow and rapid. She clutched his shoulders and squeezed her eyes tightly, reveling in yearning, yet yearning for more.

All at once he broke from the kiss and, with his other hand, clasped the back of her neck. He held her head close to him and whispered roughly in her ear. "I want ye, Alisoune. Damn, how I want ye."

"Then take me," she sobbed.

He hesitated a long moment, then at last seemed to surrender. "All right, lass. I will. But not in the bath. 'Twill be better in the bed."

She nodded, giving him one last kiss of promise. Then she struggled up and stepped out of the tub, dripping as she stood before him. But she wasn't cold, not with the way Lachlan was staring at her.

In wet linen, she might as well have been naked. Hunger burned in Lachlan's smoky eyes as he perused her. He made a sound that was half-groan, half-sigh, a sound that felt as if it generated a sympathetic vibration in all her bones.

He pulled himself out of the water, using the bracket she'd made for him. As she gazed at him standing before her—tall and massive and muscled—she was struck by a sudden shiver of fear.

He'd seemed smaller somehow in the tub, smaller and less threatening. Now he looked like a great Roman statue...except none of the statues she'd seen were quite so...endowed.

He must have sensed her trepidation. Dropping his

gaze, he lowered himself to sit on the bed and draped the sheepskin coverlet over his lap. "If ye don't want to—"

"Oh, nae!" she hurried to say. "'Tisn't that. I do. 'Tis only..."

He sighed. "My leg."

"Nae!"

"'Tis all right," he said, shaking his head. "I don't expect—"

"'Tisn't your leg," she assured him. "'Tis your...your..." She made a gesture like a caber-tosser casting a 20-foot caber, and she saw him stifle a smile.

"Oh, lass, if that's all 'tis," he said, his eyes brightening, "come here and let me soothe your fears."

He did more than soothe her. He was tender and patient, riling up her senses until she was practically begging for his touch. Then he held her close against him as they reclined together on their sides, face-to-face, flesh to flesh. Slowly and gently, with one guiding hand upon her buttocks, he pressed into her.

She sucked in a quick breath as a sharp, brief pain knifed through her.

His whisper in her ear was taut with passion. "I'm sorry, lass. It couldn't be helped. But 'twill get better, I promise."

The pain receded in a moment as he smoothed the wrinkles from her brow with his thumb. And then she only felt deliciously full.

He began to move within her, grazing her with long, easy strokes that tamed her the way that petting tamed a wild cat. For a while, 'twas pleasurable, a lovely friction

that warmed her and wrapped her head in a comforting haze. An indescribable love for him washed over her, a love for this broken man who had bared his body and his soul to her.

But gradually her fondness for him became much more. His touch no longer soothed her, but aroused her. Affection became desire. 'Twas a smoldering coal lodged betwixt her legs that suddenly sparked like a flint, a coal that he coaxed to flame.

Her mind floated away. 'Twas a purely visceral experience, and for once she was without a thought in her busy brain. Her limbs tangled with his. Primitive groans of joy came from deep within her. And her heart beat to a strange new rhythm of desire.

When she peered at him through half-closed lids, the beautiful anguish on his face catapulted her to new heights of passion, and her heart swelled in her breast.

"Oh, Lachlan!" she cried.

"Almost, love...almost."

She didn't know what he meant until she suddenly felt a tiny pinpoint of light arise inside her at the place where they were joined. It brightened as it grew, spreading out like a pool of warm honey, bathing her flesh.

He nuzzled her ear, sending a shiver of lust through her as he breathed, "Aye, lass, let it come."

And then, like a molten fount bursting up through the earth, she erupted with a throaty cry, shuddering with sweet relief.

He followed her soon after, roaring his ecstasy against

her cheek as he clung tightly to her and trembled with a forceful release.

She didn't mean to burst into tears. It just happened.

Still breathing raggedly, Lachlan caught her face in his hands and frowned in concern. "What's wrong, sweetheart?"

"'Twas beautiful," she breathed, overcome with emotion.

He smiled. "Oh, aye."

"And I just," she squeaked out between sobs, "Oh, I love ye, Lachlan."

She thought his eyes filled, too, but she'd never know for certain, because he pulled her close, cradling her head against his chest and holding her there for a long while.

Her last thought before she relaxed into the arms of slumber was whether he could learn to love her as well.

In the mellow aftermath of lovemaking, Lachlan drifted off with Alisoune in his arms. Moved by her heart's confession and filled with peace and relief, he slept more soundly than he had since the war.

'Twas morn when he next opened his eyes. What he saw in the dim light made him smile. Alisoune was sitting at the foot of the bed with a sheet draped over one shoulder, looking like a Roman goddess in spectacles. She was feasting on sugared almonds and inspecting a piece of his armor.

"Good morn," he croaked.

"Oh!" She gave a guilty start and dropped the greave, which clattered on the floor.

He smiled as she picked it up and propped it against the wall. "Did ye sleep well?"

She nodded, handing him the bag of almonds, and he popped a few in his mouth. He found her sudden shyness adorable. Also adorable were her sleep-mussed tresses, her delicate naked shoulder, and her bare feet.

"I haven't slept so well in a long while," he volunteered, reaching out a hand to entwine her fingers in his.

She nodded again, but averted her eyes, running an idle finger over the back of his hand. "Was that the first time…I mean…have you ever…"

He almost choked on an almond. He didn't know whether to be pleased or insulted that Alisoune believed he might be a virgin. "Nae, I've had a wee bit of experience." Though he'd left his wild days behind, he'd enjoyed the favors of at least a dozen maids in his youth.

"Were ye…married?"

He hesitated. Alisoune was the most curious lass he'd ever met. But he wanted to be honest with her. "Nae, but I was betrothed once."

She seemed to consider his words. "What was her name?"

"Margaret." 'Twas the first time he'd said her name out loud since she'd left. 'Twasn't as painful as he'd expected.

"What happened to her?"

Her question was a reminder that, as with Margaret,

his time with Alisoune was likely limited. "She left."

"Why?"

He sniffed. "She needed to wed a *real* man." Those had been her words, but they felt like his legacy now.

"What?" Alisoune furrowed her brows in righteous indignation. "But ye *are* a real man."

"She needed a man who wasn't a cripple, who could support her, protect her, give her a life."

"Hmph! It sounds like Margaret was the cripple."

Her assessment surprised and pleased him. Margaret *had* always been a rather helpless lass.

Alisoune rubbed the pad of her thumb across his knuckles, and her eyes turned soft. "I think she was a fool to let ye get away."

He swallowed hard. 'Twould be easy to fall under Alisoune's enchantment, because a part of him so desperately wanted to believe it. He wanted to believe, as she'd sworn last night, that she loved him. But he suspected the lass was confusing lust for love.

She'd tire of him once the novelty of lovemaking wore off. And when that happened, she'd realize he was only a helpless cripple who could do nothing for her.

Once the storm passed, she'd leave him, just as Margaret had and just as fate decreed.

But until then, he yearned to wring every drop of joy he could out of the time they had together. He might not have a future with her, but at least he'd have a sweet memory of her to warm his lonely nights.

"Lachlan?" She was drawing lazy figure eights on his thigh.

"Mm?"

"Would you want to...that is...if 'tisn't too much trouble..."

"Aye?"

She lifted her eyes to him, and he read her lusty request in their smoky green depths.

They needed no words. He grew instantly hard, she tossed aside her spectacles and her sheet, and they enjoyed a spirited breakfast in bed.

An hour later, the storm was in full-force outside. Wind whistled through the cracks between the window panes and rattled the door against its jamb.

The sound was music to Lachlan's ears. As long as the storm continued, Alisoune would remain with him. They could live in a blissful utopia and never face harsh reality.

Indeed, after their fourth bout of lovemaking, he decided he didn't care if the snow lasted till June.

CHAPTER 13

For two days, between snuggling with Lachlan under the covers, letting him bathe her in his great tub, and inventing novel positions for her new favorite pastime, Alisoune worked on a secret project.

With the snowstorm raging outside, they were stuck indoors. As Alisoune had explained to Lachlan, she'd go mad if she didn't give her active brain something to do.

And so, inspired by the sketches she'd seen by Ambroise Paré, she tinkered away on a new invention. But since she wanted to surprise Lachlan, she worked on it out of his sight behind the bed, giving him stern instructions that he wasn't allowed to peek.

Meanwhile, Lachlan kept busy, doing repairs he claimed he'd let go too long. He mixed clay to seal up the cracks around the window. He stitched up the clothing he'd let turn to rags. He washed his bed linens and hung them near the fire to dry.

A few last rivets, a bit of finessed carving, and some

strategic padding, and Alisoune finished the project. By afternoon, she was ready to let Lachlan try it out.

At least that was what she intended.

But once she saw what he'd been doing for the past half-hour—shaving off his unruly beard, revealing his chiseled jaw and square face—she thought he looked more handsome than ever, handsome and irresistible. And she didn't feel much like resisting.

Lachlan awoke in the morn with Alisoune's tangled hair draped across his face. He smiled and inhaled deeply, loving the scent of woman, the scent of *her.*

Numerous times last night she'd made him glad he'd trimmed his beard. She'd brushed her knuckles along his cheek, marveling at its smoothness, and lavished kisses all over his chin. And then, with a lascivious growl, she'd pulled his head to her bosom, inviting him to nuzzle her breasts with his freshly shaved face. That wasn't all he nuzzled, and she'd been thrilled with the erotic adventure he'd taken her on.

That they'd missed supper was little surprise. And with Campbell's uncanny ability to come and go out of the cottage on his own, the hound hadn't awakened them in the night to be let outdoors. So the fact that neither of them had stirred until now wasn't unexpected.

What *was* unexpected was what Lachlan saw when he gently brushed Alisoune's hair from his face. A bright, cheery beam of sunlight streamed in through the window and pooled on the flagstones.

His heart sank.

The storm was over.

He'd known this hour would come. Indeed, he counted himself fortunate to have had this much time with her. He didn't deserve her, after all. Women like Alisoune and Margaret were too fine for a man with one leg and no future.

Still, knowing all that didn't make it any less painful. He'd lived in denial for days now. He'd allowed himself to forget he was a cripple. He'd convinced himself her love for him would never fade. He'd let himself believe they could go on living like this in his cottage forever.

'Twas a hard delusion to give up.

Before Alisoune even opened her eyes, she stretched and yawned with cat-like grace. Smiling, she made a sound of lazy bliss, then purred, "Good morn, handsome."

His heart felt as if it might break. But he wouldn't disappoint her. If this was to be their last morn together, he'd make it one to remember.

"Good morn, beautiful," he choked out.

She cupped his chin and grinned. "I have to say I like this new face o' yours."

"Do ye now?"

"Aye. I quite like it." She gave him a lusty perusal. "I particularly like it betwixt my—"

Campbell chose that opportunity to shove his shaggy head between them and lick at Lachlan's newly bare face.

"Ach, dog!" he said in annoyance, wiping his face with the back of his hand. "Away!"

Alisoune laughed. Then she popped up, her attention

already distracted. "Oh! I never got to show ye what I've been workin' on."

Lachlan furrowed his brows. He didn't want to see it. Whatever she'd made for him, 'twould be a parting gift, something she'd leave behind that would remind him of their last hours together.

"Ach, lass, let's eat first," he said instead. "I'm starvin' to death. Ye never fed me supper last night."

She swatted playfully at his shoulder. "Am I your cook now?" Then she wiggled her eyes suggestively. "And by the way, I think ye're wrong. I recall ye had quite a nice feast last night." Then, shocked by her own lewd remark, she covered her mouth and erupted into giggles.

He smiled back, but his heart was aching. How he'd miss the sound of her laughter. "I never realized ye were such a naughty lass."

"It must be the company I keep," she teased.

He'd achieved his aim, at least for the moment. They'd have one last meal together ere he let her walk out of his life forever.

Alisoune bustled about the kitchen, cracking eggs and stirring porridge, preparing breakfast as if nothing were wrong. But if he'd looked closer, Lachlan would have noticed that her smile was shaky and her hands trembled.

She'd seen the sunlight flooding through the window.

The storm had passed.

Lachlan would expect her to leave.

And she didn't want to go. Not yet.

She loved him. She knew she'd said so in the heat of passion. But even now, with her brain fully engaged and her lust held at arm's length, 'twas true. She loved Lachlan.

She loved the way his silver eyes turned molten with desire. She loved the way he frowned in concentration when he was banking the fire. She loved how he romped with his dog, how his teeth gleamed when he smiled, how he raked the hair back from his brow.

Most of all, she loved the way he made her feel. Around Lachlan, she felt desirable and clever and beautiful. He took an interest in her interests and never appeared bored or irritated or dismissive when she spoke at length on some fine point of science that anyone else would find dull.

He appreciated her intellect, and he didn't mind her spectacles. He shared her sense of humor, and he thought her breasts were just the right size. He was amused by her sense of curiosity, and he seemed pleased by her willingness to learn when it came to lovemaking.

But she'd barely begun wooing him. If she wanted him to fall in love with her, she needed more time. She cursed the arrival of the sun, wishing 'twould disappear and not return for months.

She knew she shouldn't overstay her welcome. Lachlan had already been more than generous with his lodging, his food, his protection.

But if he could only realize how much more she had to give, how much love she could lavish upon him, how much better his life would be with her in it...

Maybe her gift would help. Maybe once he saw what she'd made for him—this unique gift of restoration given from her heart—he'd fall in love with her.

She tried to keep up a merry attitude all through breakfast, but she could see that he too seemed ill-at-ease. He was probably trying to think of how to politely ask her to leave.

She couldn't give him that opportunity. She had to keep him preoccupied—with conversation, with her gift, with her body, if necessary—to keep him from saying the words that would banish her from his cottage, and his heart, for good.

But in one of her rare quiet moments as they ate, Lachlan nodded to his hound, who was curled up in a patch of sunlight on the floor. "Campbell's missed the sun."

The porridge stuck in her throat. She had half-hoped he wouldn't notice the change in weather. Now his words, spoken aloud, seemed to hang like an ax over her head.

She rushed to fill in the deadly silence. "An interestin' thing about that... Leonardo would say the sun is a form o' *direct* light. But what we're actually seein' in the cottage isn't the sun. 'Tis *diffused* light, because it's passin' through the atmosphere." She glanced feverishly around the room, looking for something to make her point. Then she tossed her napkin onto the table and scraped back her chair, standing to pick up the stone from the mantel and holding it in the sunlight. "The light passin' through an object like this milky stone is a

different kind altogether, and the fourth," she said, turning the stone until it cast a violet wedge on her palm, "is *reflective* light, the kind that bounces off the prism in the midst o' the stone."

She knew she was chattering, but she couldn't seem to stop herself. There was a sad cast to Lachlan's eyes that told her he well understood the significance of the sun, and it had nothing to do with Leonardo da Vinci.

The porridge sat like a heavy lump in her stomach now. She didn't want him to tell her to leave. She didn't want him to say anything.

In a cheerful panic, she rushed over to snatch the cloth cover from the project she'd been working on for the past two days. She hefted up the heavy thing, brought it over, and placed it in his arms, giving him a watery smile.

He frowned at it. "What's this?"

"A gift."

"But what is it?" He turned it over.

"'Tis called a prosthesis."

"That's my armor."

"Aye, but 'tis more than that." She took it back carefully from him and demonstrated. "Above the greave and inside the poleyn is a knee hinge with a dowel that runs down to the foot, the saboton, and at the ankle, there's a spring." She took the padding out and tipped it so he could look down the top. "See the wooden top there? I took the liberty o' makin' a mold o' your leg while ye were sleepin', and I carved the wood so it should fit. But o' course, ye'll want to keep the paddin' in for comfort's sake. And then these buckles here are made to attach to your swordbelt to hold it on."

"'Tis a leg."

"Well..." She blushed. "'Tisn't quite a leg. But it should serve ye well enough. I copied the design from Paré, who—"

"Ye made me a leg."

She bit her lip, feeling strangely unsure of herself. Honestly, she couldn't tell from his expression whether he was pleased or appalled.

CHAPTER 14

Lachlan had never felt so conflicted.

Moved by Alisoune's kindness and generosity, he felt his throat close with emotion. He was overwhelmed by her gesture and impressed by her invention, which, upon closer examination, appeared to be a spectacular creation of rivets and springs and hinges that faithfully replicated the movements of a real leg.

Yet how could he accept such a gift? His limb had been the price he'd paid for outliving his brothers. He'd willingly suffered that loss, knowing they had lost so much more. 'Twasn't right that he be restored, that his debt to them be so easily forgiven.

He didn't expect her to understand. How could she? She'd never been a soldier. She didn't have brothers to look after. She didn't know the guilt he carried for surviving the battle.

"Thank ye," he murmured, setting the piece aside.

"Aren't ye goin' to try it?" she ventured.

"Later," he lied. "I'm a bit...weary now."

Her smile faltered. "Weary?" Her voice cracked on the word, and for a moment she looked uncertain. But then she tucked her lip under her teeth and stepped closer to walk her fingertips lightly up his arm. "Well, if ye're weary," she whispered in invitation, taking off her spectacles, "maybe we should go back to bed."

'Twas what he wanted more than anything—one last chance to hold her in his arms, to join with her in that most intimate of embraces, before he had to set her free.

Their mating was bittersweet—gentle yet fierce, languorous yet desperate. He tried to memorize every detail, tried to fix her image in his mind. And then he tried, unsuccessfully, to let her go.

They were still entangled a few hours later when she finally nudged him and murmured, "Come on, lazybones. I want to see how your prosthesis works."

"I'm sure it works fine."

She poked him. "Ah, Lachlan, don't be a tease. Ye know I want to see it."

"Maybe later."

"Later? What do ye mean, later?"

"Later, after ye're..."

"After I'm...?"

"Just...later." He lowered his eyes. He couldn't bear to see her hurt.

"After I'm gone," she murmured. "That's what ye were goin' to say, wasn't it?" He could hear the pain in her voice. "Ye want me gone."

"I didn't say that."

"Ye didn't have to." She turned away from him in the bed, but he could see her shoulders tense.

"Ah, ye know 'twas never meant to be, lass." He said it for his own benefit as much as hers. "*We* were never meant to be. Ye'll find a man one day, a *whole* man who will—"

"Ye *are* a whole man," she insisted.

"A man who can provide for ye, protect ye, give ye a proper life." He scowled. The thought of Alisoune with another man left a sour taste in his mouth.

She bristled at that, turning toward him with angry, tear-filled eyes. "I built ye a brace, made ye a wood and water carrier, and designed ye a prosthesis. Do ye think I need a man to provide for me? My parents left me their spectacle trade, which I've managed on my own for the last year. I'm not exactly helpless."

"I meant no insult. 'Tisn't that ye can't provide for yourself. But ye shouldn't *have* to." He rolled onto his back and stared at the ceiling. "Ye deserve better."

Alisoune's throat ached from holding back sobs. Better? She wasn't going to find better.

But she saw through his words. He pretended that her leaving was for her own good, but she knew the truth. He was only being polite to spare her feelings. He obviously didn't love her the way she loved him. And he didn't want to tell her that.

There was nothing she could do about it. She'd tried every weapon in her arsenal. She'd transformed his cottage into a warm home. She'd created tools he could

use to improve the quality of his life. She'd made him laugh. She'd even given him the gift of her body.

But 'twas impossible to force a person to feel an emotion that didn't exist inside them. Love wasn't a hypothesis, to be proved or disproved by scientific fact, but neither was it something that could be altered by alchemy. If Lachlan didn't love her, there was nothing she could do to change that.

She got out of bed before he could hear the sob in her chest and see the stricken tears in her eyes. Gathering her discarded clothing, she dressed quickly, trying not to think about her breaking heart.

Even the hound knew something was awry, for he sat alert, keeping his distance and whining softly.

She couldn't blame Lachlan...for any of it. She'd burst into his cottage, after all. She'd imposed herself upon him. It had been her idea to kiss him and, ultimately, to make love to him. She'd instigated everything. He'd only followed her lead.

Behind her, she heard him rise from the bed and pull on his trews. She brushed a tear from her cheek with her thumb. With trembling fingers, she combed her hair into a rough semblance of order and gathered her things into her satchel.

"Ye'll need food," he said behind her.

"I'm not hungry."

"'Tis a long journey."

"I'll be fine."

He sighed. "At least let me pack ye some oatcakes and cider." He limped toward the cupboard.

Then she remembered—her tools, her coin, her clothing, everything she owned was locked in her room at the Keirfield inn. She couldn't just leave them behind. She might be able to travel home to Stirling, 'Twas only six or seven miles. But without her tools and with no coin, she wouldn't survive long there.

Her shoulders slumping, she pushed the spectacles up on her nose. She didn't want to impose any further on Lachlan. But she didn't know what else to do.

"I hate to trouble ye," she said quietly, "but I can't leave quite yet. All my things…"

"They're in Keirfield?"

She nodded.

"I'll fetch them."

"Thank ye."

Their talk was so stilted, 'twas hard to believe that only an hour before, they'd been in bed together, locked in a lovers' embrace.

He continued to assemble food for her as if he provisioned her for a pilgrimage.

Campbell ambled up with his head lowered, and Alisoune scratched him behind the ears. Her eyes grew moist. She'd miss the silly hound as well.

Once Lachlan finished packing the fare and knotting it into a great linen cloth, he threw on his shirt and doublet and began tugging on his boot.

Determined not to cry, the most Alisoune could muster was a wee hopeful smile as she held out the prosthesis to him. "Maybe ye can try out your new leg on the way to Keirfield."

He paused in his labors, sighed, then resumed them. "I can't accept it."

"What?"

"The leg, I can't accept it."

"What do ye mean, ye can't accept it?"

"Maybe ye can save it for someone else."

"Someone else?" 'Twouldn't fit anyone else. Besides, 'twasn't as if one-legged men were around every corner. "But I made it for *ye*."

"I don't need it."

She flinched. "Ye're not even goin' to try it?" All the hours she'd spent customizing the armor—measuring the steel plate, carving the wood, adjusting the spring tension—and he was refusing it? She felt crushed.

He hastened to assure her, "'Tis brilliant. Ye should show it to one o' those brainy scientist fellows o' yours."

"But why wouldn't ye...?" she choked out. "I mean, I made it for ye...to make your life better."

"That's just it," he muttered under his breath as he wrenched up his boot the rest of the way. "Maybe my life shouldn't be better."

She blinked. "What in the name o' Pythagoras are ye talkin' about? Don't ye want to be happy?"

"'Tisn't a matter o' what I want. 'Tis a matter...a matter o' what I deserve."

"What?" she said, incredulous. "Why wouldn't ye deserve to be happy?"

He slipped the crutch under his arm. "Ye wouldn't understand."

"I might understand."

"Nae, ye can't," he said, pulling himself up. "Ye're not a soldier."

She crossed her arms. "I'm not a dog either, but that doesn't stop me from knowin' what pleases Campbell."

"That's different."

"How?"

"Damn it! Dogs are their own creatures. They only look after themselves. They don't have a...a king to fight for or...or fellow soldiers to watch over. They don't have young men entrustin' them with their lives!"

His voice cracked, and for an instant, she thought he might break down. But he steeled his jaw and stared at the flagstones. Eventually, his eyes grew distant with memory.

When he finally spoke, his voice was as bleak and chilling as the edge of a sharp sword. "The battle where I lost my leg, the battle at Haddon Rig, they said we won it. 'Twas a great victory for King James." He shook his head. "Not for me. My four brothers were killed in that battle. I should have been killed as well." He sniffed. "But nae, that would have been too easy. Better to leave me alive, lamed and worthless, to suffer." He frowned. "My father bid me watch over them. I failed. Because o' me, all o' my brothers are dead. And I have to atone for that."

Alisoune swallowed hard. She didn't know what to say. To lose four brothers in one battle...

"So ye see why I cannot accept your pros-..."

"Prosthesis," she breathed.

"'Tis my penance." He turned aside and hobbled off to fetch his cloak. "Payment for their souls."

Her jaw dropped. Surely he didn't believe that.

"'Twasn't your fault they were killed," she said, "was it?"

"I made a vow to my father to keep them safe."

"A vow impossible to keep. How could ye watch o'er anyone in the chaos of a battle?"

He punched the wall suddenly with the side of his fist, snarling in frustration. "I could have! I could have saved them. I could have clapped them in irons or...or ordered them home...or gotten them too drunk to stand. If I'd kept them from the fightin'...they'd still be alive."

"And they'd hate ye for keepin' them from the fightin'."

"Maybe. But they'd be *alive* to hate me."

"Ye can't blame yourself, Lachlan," she insisted. "'Twasn't your fault. Even your brothers wouldn't condemn ye. I'm sure ye did your best to protect them. What ye're feelin'—all this guilt and sufferin' as if ye're somehow to blame... Can't ye see? 'Tis like your phantom pain. 'Tisn't real."

"Ye don't know that. Ye can't know that."

"Your penance and sufferin' is not goin' to bring them back, Lachlan, any more than wishin' for your leg will grow ye a new one." She approached him cautiously and offered him the prosthesis again. "The best gift ye can give your brothers is to live your own life."

He shook his head as his eyes filled with tears. "I can't. I don't deserve a new leg." He snatched the cloak from its peg and flung open the door. "And I sure as hell don't deserve ye."

With that, he set out at a limp for Keirfield, slamming the door shut behind him.

Lachlan's sight blurred as he headed for the village. He wiped away a rogue tear that rolled down his cheek.

Alisoune's words haunted him all the way to town. *'Twasn't your fault.* How could his brothers' deaths not be his fault? He was the eldest. He was supposed to look after them.

And yet she'd stumbled upon the truth. 'Twould have been almost impossible to keep his brothers from the fighting. The Mar lads were brave and brawny, and their father had raised them up to be warriors. Sooner or later, whether Lachlan willed it or not, they'd have taken up arms in some war or another.

Then why did he feel so guilty? Why couldn't he accept their loss as just a casualty of war? Was it only because he hadn't been killed with them?

Maybe Alisoune was right. Maybe all his suffering was like his phantom pain—a cruel trick of his mind.

By the time he reached the inn in Keirfield, paid her bill, and collected her things, he decided it didn't matter if he blamed himself or not. Alisoune was leaving, taking away his only hope of happiness.

Halfway home, his leg began to throb. Remembering how Alisoune had said that cold triggered the pain, he took the liberty of digging a few rags out of her things to stuff into the knotted knee of his trews, hoping to insulate his leg against the cold.

It seemed to help, but 'twas still a long journey home. He didn't arrive at his cottage until well into the afternoon. And when he opened the door, the sight that met him made a hard lump form in his throat.

Alisoune was fast asleep, curled up on the floor in front of the hearth with her arms around his hound. Campbell raised his eyes when he saw his master, but didn't lift his head, seeming to know not to disturb the lass. Lachlan smiled ruefully, wondering which of them would be more upset when she left.

Not wishing to trouble her, he closed the door carefully behind him and quietly added a log to the fire. Then he sat on the bed with his bottle of sack, gazing down at her.

She was so beautiful to him now. He no longer saw her as a gawky, awkward, skinny lass, but as a lovely, kind, desirable woman. His heart ached when he thought about her walking out of his cottage door and never coming back.

For that reason perhaps, he felt in no hurry to wake her, instead letting his eyes drink their fill of her as she slept. He took several pulls of the sack, hoping to numb the pain—of his leg and his heart. And because she lay there for so long, with Campbell snoring beside her, perfectly content to let her remain there, Lachlan himself grew drowsy watching them slumber. Before he knew it, he was fast asleep.

CHAPTER 15

"I saw Mar leave town not an hour ago," the secretary confided to Father Ninian, arching a smug brow. "I learned from the innkeeper that he paid the woman's bill and gathered her things."

The father tapped thoughtfully at his pursed lips. When the secretary had come to him with the tale of Mar and the spectacle-seller copulating in the snow, he'd dismissed it as the ravings of the man's overactive imagination. After all, according to Margaret's last confession, Lachlan Mar was incapable of such things.

But now the issue with the spectacle-seller had become complicated in ways the secretary wouldn't understand.

"'Twould be a failin' on my part were I to allow her to spread her heresy to other villages," the father said.

The secretary nodded. "Oh, aye."

That was what he claimed—that he feared she might infect other towns with her ideas. But the truth was more

personal than that.

He'd expected the furor caused by the woman's impious ravings to have died down by now. After all, he'd run her out of town, and no one had seen her in days.

But this morn he'd overheard several of his flock *still* discussing her claim—the claim that that mad Prussian Copernicus had put forth about the Sun being the center of the galaxy—as if such a heretical notion might have true merit.

And if the townspeople started questioning the nature of the universe, 'twouldn't be long before they began to question the nature of God and, more significantly, the role of priests in such a world. Father Ninian held a certain comfortable authority in Keirfield, and he couldn't afford to lose it because of a spectacle-seller...a spectacle-seller, for God's sake!

"Why, even the woman's trade is an insult to the church," he decided, stroking his flabby chin. "Imagine the effrontery—claimin' to correct the vision that God gave us, as if 'twas somehow less than perfect."

"What will ye do, Father?" the secretary asked eagerly.

Father Ninian steepled his fingers as if in pious thought, and then sighed. "What I should have done before. God's will. Purify the heathen witch with holy fire." He made the sign of the cross. "An example must be made of her. 'Tis up to the church to prove that science is the handmaiden o' the devil, that anyone who dares challenge the will o' God must face the flames o' purification."

"But how will ye fetch her? The soldier—"

"He's a cripple," he scoffed. "By the time he comes hoppin' to intercede, the deed will be done."

The secretary rubbed uncertainly at his throat. His recent unpleasant altercation with Mar had apparently left him shaken. "And the hound?"

The priest shrugged. "Toss him breakfast—meat spiced with belladonna."

He didn't much care for dogs. They were often depicted as consorts of the devil. True, Mar might well starve without his hound's hunting skills. But that would be in the hands of God. The man probably should have died alongside his brothers on the battlefield anyway.

The first thing Lachlan noticed when he woke the next morn was the cold. He opened his eyes to see that the door stood half-open.

"Campbell," he muttered to himself. A chill wind had slipped in like a thief, stealing all the warmth from the cottage.

Then he sat up and saw that Alisoune was gone.

His heart sank to the pit of his stomach. He'd known the lass was leaving. Hell, he'd sent her away himself. Still, 'twas a blow to discover she'd left with no word of farewell...and no kiss goodbye.

They'd parted on bitter words. He wished he'd made peace with her before she left. It wouldn't change anything. She'd still be walking out of his life forever. But at least her last memory of him would be pleasant.

With a heavy heart, he rose from the bed, using the brace that every morn from now on would remind him of Alisoune.

He adored her, he realized. 'Twas absurd. He hardly knew her. But in a harsh and stifling world where a man was judged, not by his measure, but by an accident of warfare, Alisoune, who took him as he was, was a breath of fresh air.

He wedged the crutch under his arm. Then he happened to glance toward the kitchen. Alisoune's satchel and the bundle of food he'd prepared for her were still there.

His foolish heart flipped over. She hadn't left yet after all. Perhaps she'd only gone outside with Campbell. Cursing himself for having false hope—after all, she *was* leaving, whether 'twas now or later—he nonetheless hobbled eagerly to the door and opened it wider.

As he squinted against the sun-bright snow, he could make out the dark shape of his dog several yards in front of the cottage. It looked like the deerhound was stretched out on the icy slope.

"Campbell?" He frowned. "Campbell!"

The hound barely lifted his head, but wouldn't come. That wasn't like him at all. Something was wrong.

"Campbell!" he yelled, limping toward the dog as fast as he could.

God's wounds! What had happened to his beloved hound? Had he been gored by a stag? Charged by a boar? Attacked by wolves?

Halfway there, he could see Campbell's heaving sides

and the clouds of mist he huffed out with each labored breath.

"I'm comin', lad!" he called out. "Hold on! I'm comin'!"

But his crutch slipped on a patch of melting snow, and it went out from under him. He fell hard on his hip, and it took him a full minute of cursing to get his limbs under him again and retrieve the crutch.

By the time he got to Campbell, the poor beast couldn't lift his head at all. He was quaking, and his pupils were reduced to pinpoints. Beside him on the ground was a small pile of dark berries. Lachlan didn't know what they were, but his gut told him 'twas no mistake they were there. Someone had poisoned his dog.

Biting back a snarl of anger, he patted the dog's neck and murmured, "Ye'll be fine, lad."

He hoped he was right. If anything happened to Campbell...

He clenched his jaw, trying not to think about it. Nothing would happen to Campbell. He'd make sure of it.

Yet that was what he'd thought about his brothers. He'd been certain he could keep them from harm. He'd been wrong.

Still, he couldn't let fear make a coward of him. Choking down dread, he forced himself to reason.

First he had to get his dog inside where 'twas warm. Fortunately, the wood carrier Alisoune had made for him would be useful for that.

Loading the big limp hound onto it was no easy feat, but he finally managed and was able to drag Campbell back toward the cottage. All the while as he trudged

through the snow, an unthinkable question teased at the edges of Lachlan's mind. Where was Alisoune?

Just before he entered the cottage, his gaze snagged on a reflective object in the snow near the threshold. A small half-circle of broken glass stuck out of the white drifts.

His breath caught in his chest. Alisoune's spectacles. They were broken.

She wouldn't have been so careless. And she'd never go anywhere without her spectacles.

Not willingly.

All at once, he knew what had happened. His heart began to pound like the drums of war.

Steeling his nerves as best he could, he wrapped Campbell in blankets near the fire and put a bowl of water nearby. But a dire thought kept echoing through his brain... If they'd poisoned Campbell, what had they done to Alisoune?

He was afraid he knew the answer, what they'd intended all along—to burn her at the stake.

For the love of God, he had to save her. But there was no time. And the devils who'd taken her had known that. They'd poisoned his dog, but they hadn't bothered waylaying *him*, because they knew a one-legged man was no match for them. They'd be done with their unholy business before he could even limp into Keirfield.

Seething with rage and frustration, Lachlan pounded his fist against the hearth, knocking the round stone from the mantel. It fell and rolled to a stop beside Campbell.

With a curse, he threw his useless crutch across the

room. It clattered over the flagstones and landed at the foot of the steel leg Alisoune had made for him.

At first, Alisoune had been angry with herself for falling so easily into their trap. Campbell had let himself out of the cottage, as was his morning custom, but he was gone a long while. Naturally, she ventured out to see what had become of him.

They'd caught her instantly, gagging her ere she could cry out, tying her hands behind her ere she could fight her way free. And that was when she saw that they'd also hurt Campbell, done something to make him crumple to the ground, unable to move, unable to come to her aid.

When they picked her up to carry her away, her spectacles fell off, and she heard a crunch as one of the men stepped on them. And for Alisoune, not being able to see clearly was almost as frightening as thinking about what they intended to do with her.

Now, however, anger had given way to terror. She was in Keirfield proper, where a stake had been erected and stacked with kindling in the town square. While two men held her captive before a crowd of villagers, the priest went on and on about the will of God and purifying fire. He was making no logical sense whatsoever with his strange ravings about witches and demons, the heretic Copernicus and the evils of spectacles. And then, as if his lack of logic wasn't frightening enough, all the townsfolk joined in, echoing his sentiments, embracing his condemnation of her as if 'twere an absolute truth.

If only he'd remove her gag, there were arguments she might make in her favor, scientific evidence that could prove she was no blasphemer. And yet she knew her voice would not be heard over the rabid fervor of the crowd. What men couldn't understand, they feared. And what they feared, they sought to destroy.

As helpless as she was, she couldn't quiet her feverish brain as the men sliced her dress from her, leaving her shivering in her chemise. Why, she wondered, did the priest not just let her go? She'd been planning to leave Keirfield. Surely he knew that. He'd never see her again. So why had he brought her back to burn her at the stake? Why was he so intent on killing her?

All at once, it came to her. The priest wasn't just killing her. He was killing science. Science threatened his control over these people. In the same way men believed the planets revolved around the earth, Father Ninian believed his flock revolved around him. He viewed Alisoune as an intruder who had upset what he considered the natural order of things. And the only way he could restore that order was to convince his flock that Alisoune was a witch, that science was blasphemy, that knowledge was evil.

She fought back a sob as the men wrenched her forward toward the stake.

If only she hadn't stepped outside to look for Campbell...

If only she hadn't delayed her departure, hoping Lachlan would change his mind...

If only she'd told him how much she loved him, how

she never wanted to leave him, how she knew they belonged together and how happy she would make him...

Now she'd never get the chance.

Her eyes filled with tears as they tied her to the stake and acrid smoke rose from a flaming brand.

Even if Lachlan woke to find her gone, he wouldn't be able to save her. There wouldn't be time. She'd be dead before he got halfway to Keirfield.

Lachlan's stump hurt like hell. But now that he'd mastered the steel leg, it worked like a perfectly engineered crossbow. With a naked sword in his fist and a bloodthirsty sneer on his face, he covered the mile to Keirfield in long, determined strides.

No battle had ever fired up his blood like this. No enemy had ever stirred such rancor in him. His force of will was sharpened to a fine edge, and nothing could turn aside his blade now.

When he entered the town and first beheld Alisoune—a frail angel in white bound to a blackened stake—he let out a loud roar and raised his sword.

The man holding the brand hesitated. The crowd wheeled his way. Lachlan strode forward with menace—his face grim, his manner merciless.

Suddenly, the air was filled with gasps. Mothers grabbed their children. Men staggered backward. The secretary's jaw dropped. And Father Ninian clutched his chest.

As Lachlan made his way through the parting crowd, he heard whispers of speculation around him.

"His leg's grown back…"

"'Tis a miracle…"

"The spell of a witch…"

"God's own hand…"

"The work o' Satan…"

"Impossible…"

"Bewitched…"

"Blessed…"

Lachlan didn't care what they thought. He didn't care if they believed his restored leg was a gift from God or a curse of the devil…as long as they didn't stand between him and the beautiful lass he meant to rescue and hold onto for the rest of his life.

epilogue

December 8

"Slow down!" Alisoune called after Lachlan, laughing. Now that he'd had a few weeks to practice walking on his prosthesis, he sped along the streets of Stirling as if he'd worn it all his life.

"Hurry up!" he retorted. "I want to take the stone in ere the shop gets busy."

She grinned and shook her head. She wasn't quite sure what he intended to do with the rainbow crystal. But she supposed he'd never get over the notion 'twas some sort of magical relic. When they'd returned to the cottage on that awful day the villagers had taken her to find Campbell with the stone under his paw, completely recovered from his poisoning, Lachlan claimed the old crone had been right. The Winter Stone had changed the dog's fate.

Alisoune didn't really care what he believed about the crystal. She was just happy he believed in her love and in himself again.

They'd decided to leave Keirfield forever. There was still disagreement in the town as to whether Lachlan's new leg was the work of God or the work of Lucifer. Alisoune didn't dare try to convince them 'twas just a work of engineering.

So they sold his cottage and moved into her house in Stirling. She made spectacles in her downstairs workshop. And 'twasn't long before Lachlan's skills with the sword got him work training young lads to fight.

"Here we are," he announced, tugging on Campbell's leash and stopping at the shop where a wooden sign embossed with a gold cup proclaimed it *John Gilder, Goldsmith.* Unfortunately, the door was closed. It appeared John Gilder wasn't in residence. Lachlan frowned. "Damn. Where can he have gone?"

But Alisoune was never one to make assumptions. She required empirical proof. So she banged loudly on the door. Sure enough, a few moments later, a key turned in the lock, and the door opened a crack. Out peered a lass of no more than fourteen, dressed in a blue smock. She was a bonnie young thing with dark hair, a dimpled chin, and big brown eyes.

"Is the goldsmith here?" Alisoune asked her.

The lass looked undecided for a moment. Then she nodded and opened the door wide. "Aye. Come in."

Beautiful gold pieces were displayed all around the

shop, some with jewels, some with enamels, some with pearls. The handiwork was amazing.

"I have a stone," Lachlan said, pulling it out of his coin pouch. "I'd like to have it set."

"Oh!" the lass exclaimed. "'Tis a rainbow crystal."

Alisoune lifted a smug brow at Lachlan.

"Can the goldsmith do it today?" he asked.

"Today?" the lass squeaked.

"Aye." Lachlan had gotten very superstitious about the stone. He didn't want to be without it for any more than a few hours.

"Well..." the lass said, casually reaching over to scratch Campbell behind the ears. "John Gilder is away for a few days." Her eyes lit up as she confided, "He's gone to see the new queen, to present a gift to her."

"The new queen?" Lachlan asked with a frown.

"Aye, sir. Have ye not heard?" She could barely contain her excitement. "The babe was born today. She's called Mary, after her mother."

"A lass," Alisoune said in wonder. Both England and Scotland had possible female heirs to the thrones then.

Lachlan sighed. "So it can't be done today?"

"Well..." the lass said, catching her lip under her teeth. "There *is* another goldsmith here who could do the work."

"By the end o' the day?" he asked.

"Aye, sir."

"And 'tis quality work?" he asked.

"Aye, sir." She fetched a tray full of intricate pins,

brooches, and rings. She lifted her chin as she said, "'Tis the same goldsmith who made these."

He nodded his approval. "Fine."

As he went on to describe what he wanted done, Alisoune narrowed her eyes at the lass, taking note of her apprentice's smock. Then she asked with a knowing smile, "Would ye be the goldsmith's daughter...and his apprentice?"

The lass gulped in guilt. "Foster daughter, aye. My name is Florie."

"Well, Florie," she said with a wink, "I think we'll be very pleased with the results."

As it turned out, Alisoune *was* very pleased, particularly because Lachlan had had the Winter Stone mounted into a pendant for *her*. 'Twas a wedding gift, he said, which she gleefully accepted.

If he wanted to claim that the Winter Stone gleamed bright blue with peace and contentment as he fastened it around her neck, she didn't bother arguing 'twas only the prism inside that made it so. For Lachlan, 'twas a reminder that one's destiny could be altered, that all wounds could be mended, and that love was the most powerful healer of all.

The End

ᴄhank you for reading my book!

MACFARLAND'S LASS

The Scottish Lasses Book 1

SELKIRK, SCOTLAND
SPRING 1545

The pain was shocking, intense. Florie's first thought was that a wolf had sprung at her from the brush, sinking its fangs into her thigh. She screamed, but the sound was cut off as she twisted and fell, colliding hard with the earth.

Knocked breathless, for an instant she lay stunned. Then, fearing to be devoured, she kicked desperate heels into the decaying leaf-fall, scrambling, clambering, scraping dirt beneath her nails as she struggled to escape the unrelenting burn of the teeth embedded in her flesh.

No beast snarled or sprang to finish her, but neither did the stabbing pain in her leg subside. She wrenched about to see what demon had her in its jaws.

The sight left her faint with horror.

An arrow pinned her through a trailing link of her gold girdle and her skirts, its steel head buried in her flesh, its thick shaft bobbing as she writhed in pain.

The edges of perception blurred then. She felt herself tilting, fading, falling into a cavern of seductive oblivion.

Rane's bowstring was still vibrating when the blood drained from his face and his arms dropped limp at his sides.

"Bloody hell," he breathed.

Casting off the bow, he charged forward into the open meadow, his heart hammering. He bolted for the trail, toward his fallen prey, hurtling along the pond's edge, around its perimeter, whipping past reeds and fern, snapping off bracken as he ran. When he reached his victim, he dropped his quiver to the ground and fell to his knees with a bitter cry.

Guilt threatened to unman him, and he ground his teeth against a wave of self-loathing.

Curse his hands, he'd shot a child.

Then he peered closer by the fading twilight. Nae, not a child. A slight, slender lass.

Though she lay as still as death, she wasn't dead. Thank Odin, he'd been able to redirect the arrow at the last moment, thus sparing her life.

He turned her carefully toward him, and she revived with a wheezing gasp, reflexively scrabbling at the outside of her thigh, where his arrow obscenely protruded.

"Nae!" he cautioned. "Leave it be!"

Her eyes widened, and he instantly withdrew his hands, trying not to panic her, raising his palms in what he hoped was a placating gesture.

The last thing he expected was the sting of a sharp needle through his open hand.

He grunted in pain, drawing back his wounded palm. Blood welled from the puncture. He sucked a sharp hiss through his teeth.

The needle had pierced him deeply. But he supposed he should have known better. After all, only a fool approached a wounded animal.

Her left arm arced toward him again with whatever vicious weapon she wielded.

He lunged aside. "Nae, lass! I mean ye no—"

His words were cut short as her right fist clipped his jaw.

"Ach!"

The needle returned to graze his bare neck, leaving a stinging trail.

"Son of a... Lass, cease! 'Twas an acci—"

She ignored his command, attacking him again and again, as if she intended to fight him to the death. Damn! If she didn't stop thrashing about, she'd drive the arrow deeper into her thigh.

"Woman!" he finally bellowed, startling her into momentary submission. "Put away your weapon. I'm friend, not foe."

Florie didn't believe him for an instant. Whether he was Gilbert's man she couldn't tell. 'Twas too dark to make out his face or the color of his cloak. But the villain had shot her. *Shot* her!

She'd managed to wound him with her brooch pin. She'd heard his grunt, felt the point sink into his flesh. But she hadn't inflicted enough damage to stop him. And if she didn't... If he turned her over to the law...

Fighting for her life, she stabbed forward with the brooch again. This time he was prepared for her attack. He caught her wrist in a steely grip.

Thrashing against his punishing hold, she tried to pry his fingers away with her free hand. But he gave her wrist a sharp flick, and the brooch flew loose, skittering out of reach.

"Lie still," he commanded. "Ye'll only make it worse."

Worse? What could be worse? Florie wasn't about to surrender, regardless of the wave of dizziness that assailed her...regardless of the dire stain widening on her best brocade skirts...regardless of the drops of blood, her blood, dripping onto the leaves of the forest floor.

Summoning up one last, desperate burst of power, she reared back her closed fist and swung forward as hard as she could, aiming for his jaw. But he ducked easily out of the way, seizing that hand as well.

"For the love o' Frigga, lass, lie *still!*"

The edges of her vision dimmed, darkening as her bones dissolved into submission, and she vaguely wondered who the devil Frigga was.

God have mercy. Maybe the archer had dealt her a mortal wound and she was dying, for she felt as weak as a bairn, with neither the strength nor the will to move.

"Nae, nae, nae, nae, NAE!" he shouted, giving her wrists a reviving shake. "Not *that* still!" His voice, for all its vehemence, sounded distant, dreamlike. "Stay awake, do ye hear me?"

"Ye go to hell," she mumbled.

He cursed under his breath, returning her arms to her

sides, where they lay as limp and useless as empty sleeves.

"Ach, lass," he murmured, as if to himself, "what were ye doin', stealin' through the thicket like that?"

"Leave me alone."

"If I leave ye alone, ye'll bleed to d—" He shook his head. "I'm not leavin'."

From beneath eyelids growing heavier by the moment, Florie could faintly discern the man's silhouette as he crouched nearby. He was unbuckling his belt.

Ballocks! Did the monster mean to swive her while she lay helpless?

"Get the hell away from me," she managed to croak.

He ignored her.

She heard the sound of fabric being shredded. The brute must be tearing her clothes from her. Tears of rage and frustration and anguish welled in her eyes. "Bastard," she whispered.

"Aye, I know. But 'twill be over in a moment. Lie still."

"Nae!" she groaned. She wasn't about to let the lout have his way with her. She tried to curl her weak fingers into lethal fists. "Don't touch me."

A dark fog crept in at the sides of her vision like a closing curtain. She fought to keep her eyes open.

"I'll be swift as I can," he promised, "but ye have to hold still." He positioned himself beside her injured leg. "I'll carry ye to shelter afterward. There's a priest up the rise from here, not far—"

A priest! That brought her instantly alert. "The church!" she blurted.

Sanctuary! By strength of sheer will, she seized his wrist in one hand with such ferocity that she almost knocked him off his haunches.

"Aye!" she cried, though her command came out on a weak wheeze. "The church... Go... Now..." If she could make it to the church... Pain gripped her again, and she winced, digging her fingers into the leather bracer around his forearm.

"Soon." He clasped a restraining hand over hers, his fingers sticky with blood.

"Now," she groaned. Leveraging against his wrist, she began to creep forward, determined to drag herself bodily up the hill if need be.

"Lass, be still! Ye'll drive the arrow—"

"Sanctuary!" she beseeched him.

"What?"

"Take me...to sanctuary." Lord Gilbert couldn't be far away. "They're comin'," she mumbled.

"Who?"

She gasped as searing lightning shot up her leg.

He squeezed her hand. "All right. I'll hurry, lass," he promised, "but the shaft's got to come out first." The cloth he'd torn he now rapidly wadded into his hand. Then he offered her his leather belt. "Hold this in your teeth."

She turned her head aside. She didn't want his belt. All she wanted was sanctuary.

But he pulled her jaw down with his thumb anyway, wedging the thick belt between her teeth. "Bite down."

She scowled. No one told Florie what to do. Then a strong wave of pain washed over her as he pressed the

wad of linen against her wound, and she reflexively clamped down.

Blowing out a forceful breath and kneeling above her, the man curved his right hand around the shaft so 'twas braced under his arm. "Ready?"

Nae, she wasn't ready. But Lord Gilbert was coming. And this knave wouldn't let her go until the arrow was out. Praying the brute wouldn't betray her, that he'd keep his word, she ground her teeth into his belt and nodded.

"One... two..."

She fainted before he reached three.

ABOUT THE AUTHOR

I'm a *USA Today* bestselling author of swashbuckling action-adventure historical romances, mostly set in Scotland, with over a dozen award-winning books published in six languages.

But before my role as a medieval matchmaker, I sang in *The Pinups,* an all-girl band on CBS Records, and provided voices for the MTV animated series *The Maxx,* Blizzard's *Diablo* and *Starcraft* video games, and *Star Wars* audiobooks.

I'm the wife of a rock star (if you want to know which one, contact me) and the mother of two young adults. I do my best writing on cruise ships, in Scottish castles, on my husband's tour bus, and at home in my sunny southern California garden.

I love transporting readers to a place where the bold heroes have endearing flaws, the women are stronger than they look, the land is lush and untamed, and chivalry is alive and well!

I'm always delighted to hear from my readers, so please feel free to email me at glynnis@glynnis.net. And if you're a super-fan who would like to join my inner circle, sign up at http://www.facebook.com/GCReadersClan, where you'll get glimpses behind the scenes, sneak peeks of works-in-progress, and extra special surprises!